Cru ~~p~~ ~~Christian Cozy~~
Mysteries Series

Book 10

Hope Callaghan

hopecallaghan.com
Copyright © 2017
All rights reserved.

This book is a work of fiction. Although places mentioned may be real, the characters, names and incidents and all other details are products of the author's imagination and are used fictitiously. Any resemblance to actual events or actual persons, living or dead is purely coincidental.

No part of this publication may be copied, reproduced in any format, by any means, electronic or otherwise, without prior consent from the copyright owner and publisher of this book. The only exception is brief quotations in printed reviews.

Visit my website for new releases and special offers: hopecallaghan.com

i

Acknowledgments

Thank you, Peggy H., Jean P., Cindi G., Wanda D. and Barbara W. for taking the time to preview *High Seas Heist,* for the extra sets of eyes and for catching all of my mistakes.

A special thanks to my reader review team: Alice, Amary, Barbara, Becky, Becky B, Brinda, Cassie, Christina, Debbie, Denota, Devan, Grace, Jan, Jo-Ann, Joeline, Joyce, Jean K., Jean M., Kathy, Lynne, Megan, Melda, Kat, Linda, Lynne, Pat, Patsy, Paula, Renate, Rita, Rita P, Shelba, Tamara and Vicki.

CONTENTS

Chapter 1

The weight of the week ahead lay heavy on Millie Sanders' mind as she stepped inside the Siren of the Seas' atrium and slowly gazed around.

Within the hour, passengers would begin boarding the mega cruise ship while Millie's boss, Andy Walker, was on a plane on his way back to the UK, leaving Millie, the assistant cruise director, in charge.

The ship had been out of commission and in dry dock for a week while an army of workers completed major renovations. The renovations included adding a rock-climbing wall, revamping the ship's buffet area, adding cantilever hot tubs and sprucing the place up.

Before Andy left, he and Millie met to go over scheduling and the next two weeks entertainment. He'd even given her a special phone number, a "hotline" to reach him in the event of an actual emergency.

Despite Andy's assurance she was more than capable of filling in for him, they were big shoes to fill. She squeezed her eyes shut and offered up a small prayer for a week of smooth sailing with no major crises.

"You okay?" Millie felt a light tap on her shoulder and turned to face Donovan Sweeney, the ship's purser.

"I'm praying."

Donovan chuckled. "C'mon Millie. You'll be fine. Andy left you in charge of the ship's entertainment for good reason. You're more than capable of handling the job. I'll be here to help in any way that I can."

"Awesome," she teased. "I have a sequined purple body suit and matching pair of heeled tap shoes that would fit you perfectly."

"You know what I mean." Donovan glanced at his watch. "Not only am I here to offer my support, but I wanted to fill you in on the special guests who'll be on board for this week's cruise."

Millie raised an eyebrow. "Special guests?"

Donovan cleared his throat. "Ted Danvers and his family will be boarding shortly."

"Ted Danvers." The name sounded familiar...too familiar. Millie's breath caught in her throat and she began to feel lightheaded. "The CEO of Majestic Cruise Lines is going to be on our ship?"

"Yes. Mr. Danvers and his family were on board last night to check out the recent renovations and decided they wanted to cruise with us this week. Since Siren of the Seas was the first in the fleet to get the major upgrades, he wanted to get firsthand passenger feedback."

"You're kidding." Millie clutched Donovan's arm. "Tell me you're kidding."

"I'm kidding."

"Good." Millie sucked in a breath and closed her eyes.

"But I'm not. He and his family are on their way now. They'll be staying in the grand suite and I'm assigning them a personal assistant and concierge."

Donovan began massaging his temples. "After we figure out what they want to do for the week as far as specialty dining, seating for the headliner shows and activities they're interested in, I'll call a staff meeting to go over everything."

Millie had never seen the cool-as-a-cucumber Donovan appear ruffled. But Donovan was ruffled. "We need this week's cruise to go off without a hitch."

"I guess this means no dead bodies, no poisonings, no fires and no hijackings," Millie quipped.

"Absolutely not. I want this to be the most entertaining yet uneventful cruise ever. If you find a body, hide it in the closet until the cruise ends and then we'll deal with it."

Donovan rattled on, instructing Millie to be hyper-vigilant in keeping her staff under control, mainly Danielle Kneldon who had a knack for getting into trouble. He also mentioned Millie's friend, Annette Delacroix, who was the ship's director of food and beverage.

The only name Donovan didn't mention was Cat Wellington, but Cat typically only became involved in Millie's adventures when Millie dragged her into them.

She lifted her hand to her forehead and saluted. "Aye-aye, Donovan. I will be on my very best behavior."

"Good." Donovan glanced at his watch again. "I'm on my way to get an update on the status of Danvers and his family. The captain, Dave Patterson, as well as myself and you, of course, will be on hand to greet the family as they board."

"Of course," Millie nodded.

He hurried off and an inkling of dread crept through Millie's body. She could count on one hand the number of cruises that had been uneventful, even if it was only locking up an unruly, usually inebriated, passenger in the ship's holding area.

There was never a dull moment and if history were any indication, this cruise would not be any different. It wasn't a matter of "if" something would happen, but "when."

There was just enough time for Millie to meet with the entertainment staff and give them a heads up about the special guests who would be cruising with them.

She slowly descended the stairs to deck three. Millie picked up the pace as she made her way toward the stage and Andy's office, nearly colliding with Danielle, who came barreling down the stairs.

"Whoa." Millie scrambled to get out of the young woman's way. "Where's the fire?"

"Oh my gosh. You scared me half to death. I was coming to look for you."

"And I was coming to look for you," Millie said. "We need to have a quick meeting with all of the staff."

"You heard?" Danielle clutched her chest.

"Yeah. Donovan told me the Danvers family is cruising with us this week. We have to be on our game, which is why I want to have a quick chat with the staff."

Danielle shook her head. "The Danvers family is coming on our ship?"

"I thought that's what you were talking about. Donovan just told me."

"I had no idea." Danielle's eyes widened. "No. I was down on deck six, talking to Pierre about a change in location for the wine tasting event when Brenda Parcore ran out of the art gallery, screaming that one of the limited edition Romare

Tourmine paintings was missing. She's freaking out."

"As long as she freaks out downstairs and nowhere near the gangway where passengers board, I'm not gonna worry about it," Millie said. "I have enough problems."

"Unfortunately, it is kind of your problem. She was ranting and raving that the last time she saw the painting was when Andy was admiring it yesterday. She's telling everyone who will listen that she thinks Andy stole it."

Chapter 2

"That's crazy," Millie sputtered. "Andy wouldn't steal a painting, even if it was a *Picasso*. What is he gonna do? Hang it in his cabin?"

"He's not here to defend himself. She could easily accuse him of smuggling it off the ship."

"What was the stolen art worth? A couple hundred bucks?" Millie was not an art aficionado and had no idea what a Romare Tourmine painting might be worth. "I'll look into it later. We need a quick meeting and then I have to head upstairs to start greeting passengers."

The women hurried to the back of the stage and Andy's office, which, for better or for worse, was Millie's command center for the next week – or two. She secretly hoped Andy would surprise her and return the following week, instead of being gone the two weeks he'd mentioned.

Danielle offered to assemble the entertainment staff while Millie quickly reviewed the week's schedule of events. New to the lineup was the "Dress the Guest" competition on the lido deck, not to mention the popular painting party. She thought of Brenda Parcore's claim that Andy heisted an expensive painting.

As far as Millie knew, Andy had little interaction with the High Seas Gallery employees. The art dealer was a third party company who hosted the art auctions and art exhibits on board Majestic Cruise Lines' fleet of ships.

She pushed her worries over the accusations aside. Millie had issues on her mind that were more pressing.

The entertainment staff began making their way inside the small office and Millie waited until it was standing room only. "Is this everyone? Good. I'll get right to it. As you all know, Andy is off on emergency leave this week and he's left me in charge."

"And me second in command," Danielle piped up.

"Yes. Danielle will be my right hand gal. It's going to be a busy week and I want to make sure we're all on the same page as far as entertainment. I'm going to be busting my butt, working hard to fill Andy's shoes. This office will be ground zero, our command post."

Millie tapped the bulletin board on the wall behind her. "I'll post the entire week's schedule on this board."

Kevin, one of the lido deck staff, raised his hand. "Are we going to start the new headliner show *Waves of Wonder* this week?"

"Good question. No," Millie said bluntly. "I want to wait until Andy returns." She briefly ran over the week's events and spent extra time going over the sea days' schedules. Sea days were different from port days and included an extensive list of organized activities, as well as evening headliner shows. "Any more questions?"

Danielle nudged Millie. "Aren't you going to tell them?" she whispered under her breath.

"Tell them what?"

"About the Danvers family."

"Oh. I almost forgot." Millie raised her voice. "In case you haven't heard, Ted Danvers, the CEO of Majestic Cruise Lines, along with his family, will be on board the ship this week."

There was a collection of audible gasps.

"Great," Aaron, another of the dancers, groaned.

"Great as in I hope you're excited," Millie said.

Aaron shook his head. "Last fall I was working on another Majestic Cruise line ship and the Danvers family sprung a surprise visit on us." He gave Millie a quick glance.

"Go on," she urged. "I think we should all hear this."

"The woman - I think it was his wife or something, hit on me...and his son? Teddy the Terrible was a total monster."

It was the last thing Millie wanted to hear. "You said this was last year?"

"Yeah. It was right before I jumped ship and joined Siren of the Seas."

"Okay everyone," Millie said. "Let's keep Aaron's information in the back of our minds but remember that Mr. Danvers is our boss and we need to go above and beyond to prove to him that Siren of the Seas has the best crew and staff of any ship in the fleet."

The employees filed out of the room. Aaron was one of the last to leave and began to exit the office.

Millie grabbed his arm. "Hang on."

When only Danielle, Millie and Aaron were left, Millie spoke. "What's the real scoop? Did Danvers' wife actually hit on you?"

"Oh boy." Aaron shook his head. "The woman is like a prowling cougar, ready to pounce on any male within striking distance. Teddy the Terrible almost set fire to the teen lounge and destroyed one of the arcade games after he punched a hole in the Plexiglas. On the last day of the cruise, he tossed a bucket of mini golf balls over the side of the ship when someone beat him at mini golf."

"He sounds like a real doll." Danielle rolled her eyes.

"Ken, the cruise director of the ship, decided to put me in charge of 'entertaining' Teddy. It was a nightmare and he almost got me fired. He tried to pin the blame on me after he destroyed all of the basketball hoops on the sports deck. Fortunately, they caught him on video, destroying the hoops."

"Oh no." Millie's hand flew to her mouth as visions of a sullen teen bent on destroying the ship's property popped into her head.

"He's a bored, rich kid. I never once saw his parents discipline him."

"Millie, do you copy?" Millie's radio blared. It was Donovan.

She pulled her radio from her belt and pressed the side button. "Go ahead, Donovan."

"It's show time, time for you to head to the gangway to greet our passengers."

"I'm on my way." Millie clipped the radio to her belt. "So I guess if I need someone to babysit Terrible Teddy, you're not going to volunteer."

"Not on your life." Aaron led the way out of Andy's office. "I'd rather walk the plank."

Millie followed behind Aaron and Danielle brought up the rear. "I appreciate the heads up."

"Good luck," Aaron said. "You're gonna, I mean *we're* gonna need it." He walked to the changing room in the back and Millie and Danielle strode out of the stage. When they reached the hall, Danielle abruptly stopped. "Card please."

"Huh?"

"I need your special access card. Now that I'm assistant cruise director, I should have the same access you have."

"Oh no."

"Oh yes. If you want me to be your right hand gal, I need all of the benefits and privileges that go with it." Danielle held out her hand. "Or you're on your own and you can find someone else to fill in."

"You're bribing me."

"I prefer the word incentivizing. Do you want my help or not?"

"Of course I do." Millie reluctantly pulled the spare keycard Andy had given her from her front pocket and dropped it in Danielle's hand. "Do not lose this. Do not access restricted areas of the ship without prior permission. Do not..."

Danielle cut Millie off. "I won't do anything you wouldn't do," she promised.

"Great. That's what I was afraid of." The women made their way to the atrium where Donovan,

Dave Patterson, Annette and Captain Armati stood waiting for the first wave of guests to arrive.

"Hail, hail, the gang's all here," Millie said as she slid in next to Nic…Captain Armati. He squeezed her hand and winked. "How's my girl?"

Slow warmth crept from the top of Millie's head to the tips of her toes. "Better now, although check back with me in a couple days and I may be singing a different tune."

"You'll do fine." The captain released her hand as a sudden commotion near the gangway drew their attention.

"Hey!" A young man elbowed Suharto, one of the gangway security guards.

"Ompf." Suharto doubled over and clutched his stomach.

"That loser tried to trip me!" the teen shouted.

"Now Teddy." A petite, thin blonde woman teetered on stiletto heels as she attempted to soothe the dark-haired teenager. "I'm sure it was an accident."

"Teddy." A tall, muscular man with curly red hair leaned forward. "We're not even on the ship yet. Would you like to go home?"

"I would. It wasn't my idea to board this hunk of junk in the first place."

Captain Armati broke ranks and approached the trio. He extended his hand. "Mr. Danvers. It's a pleasure to see you again." He turned to the woman, who was eyeing Nic with interest. "Hello Ms…"

"Brigitte. You can call me Brigitte." The woman slowly smiled and placed her hand in Nic's hand. "Why thank you, Captain Artesian." Millie could almost hear the woman purr as she said his name, the wrong name.

"Armati," Millie muttered under her breath.

Danielle nudged her and cleared her throat.

The woman shot Millie a hard glance and turned her attention once again to Millie's betrothed. "I hear we'll be dining at the captain's table. I would love to hear all about the ship's recent renovations. Perhaps you could give me a private tour?" She batted her eyes.

Millie clenched her fists as an overwhelming urge to slap the woman filled her.

Donovan Sweeney, noting the look of rage on Millie's face, strode over. "We're thrilled you could join us on board Siren of the Seas." He turned to Danielle. "Danielle, could you please show the Danvers family to the grand suite up on deck ten?"

"Of course." Danielle hurried forward.

Brigitte thrust her carry-on bag at Danielle. "Perfect. Are you going to be my personal assistant for the week? Theodore mentioned there would be special staff assisting us during the cruise."

"Uh. No." Danielle shot Donovan a glance. "I'm sure Donovan can fill you in on special guest services." The trio followed Danielle to the set of glass elevators on the other side of the room.

Millie watched them step into the empty elevator and disappear from sight.

Suharto hurried over to Dave Patterson, the ship's head of security. "Boss. I promise I did not trip the young man. He must've caught his foot on the metal divider."

Patterson patted Suharto's shoulder. "Don't worry Suharto. We know you didn't do anything wrong."

Suharto nodded in relief and returned to his post near the gangway entrance.

Past guests began congregating in the atrium, followed by passengers with priority boarding.

Millie pasted a smile on her face as she stood next to the captain, greeting several of the passengers by name, all the while, vowing to keep a close eye on Brigitte.

Chapter 3

After the initial crush of passengers thinned,
Millie darted to the lido deck to make sure the sail
away party was underway before stopping by
guest services to calm an irate guest who insisted
on getting passes for the sold out wine and dine
mystery dinner show. Thankfully, Nikki and
Millie were able to reach Pierre LeBlanc, the
sommelier, who assured them he could fit another
table for two in the venue.

She put out two unexpected "fires" before
sneaking into the renovated *Waves* buffet to grab
a quick bite to eat. The new layout of the buffet
was near genius.

The old layout, a design that consisted of two
identical buffet areas, was cumbersome. The lines
to get to the food were long, especially during the
breakfast and lunch hours.

The ship's designers re-configured the buffet to consist of four sides. Each side offered the exact same dishes as the other three sides.

Millie made her way around the square and found only one or two people, at most, waiting in line.

The new layout also included separate soda and sparkling water stations.

Millie filled her plate with a scoop of Italian pasta salad, a hot ham and cheese sandwich, some French fries and an unidentifiable rice mixed with what looked like sausage, onion and diced green peppers.

She searched for an empty table and finally gave up before heading outdoors, to a quiet area overlooking the bustling port below.

Soon, it would be time for the mandatory safety or muster drill, a safety briefing that all passengers, crew and staff were required to attend.

She inhaled the pasta salad, ate half of her ham and cheese sandwich and sampled a bite of the rice dish. Millie made a sour face, as she tasted curry.

"That bad?" Millie's friend, Annette, placed her tray of food on the table and pulled out the chair across from her.

"I'm not a fan of curry." Millie moved the rice to the side of her plate.

"How's it going without Andy?"

Millie dipped a fry in catsup and chewed the end. "Okay, I guess. I can't believe Ted Danvers and his family are on board the ship."

"Not to mention springing it on us at the last minute." Annette tore off a piece of her roll and slathered a thick layer of butter across the top. "I've already received a detailed list of demands. French press coffee delivered at nine every morning, accompanied by Scotch eggs for Mr. Danvers and frosted cornflakes cereal with whole milk for TT."

"TT?"

"Terrible Teddy. Haven't you heard the rumors? The kid is a total brat." Annette bit her roll. "Personally, I think he's crying out for attention. I hear the woman is Danvers' fiancée."

Millie curled her lip. "She's a trip. She wants Captain Armati to give her a personal tour of the ship."

"That's probably not the only thing she wants a personal tour of."

"That's what I'm afraid of, but what can I do? Now is the perfect opportunity to ask Mr. Danvers for permission for Captain Armati and me to marry. I don't want to tick off his wife-to-be or have his son accuse me of some heinous crime."

"All we can do is keep a low profile and hope for the best."

"I can't keep a low profile. I'm in charge of entertainment. Andy couldn't have picked a better time to abandon ship," Millie moaned as she tossed her napkin on top of her uneaten food.

"I feel for ya', Millie. If there's anything I can do to help..."

"Millie, do you copy?"

"That sounds like Dave Patterson." Millie grabbed her radio. "I'm here. Go ahead."

"Yes. I'm in my office with Brenda Parcore. I wondered if you could stop by for a minute."

"Of course. I'll be right there."

"Isn't she the one who runs the art auction and art gallery?" Annette asked.

"Yep. Danielle told me she overheard Parcore claim that an expensive limited edition piece of art was missing and is blaming it on Andy."

"How convenient," Annette said. "He's not even on the ship."

"Right?" Millie shoved her chair back and stood. "I can hardly wait to hear this." She told her friend good-bye before heading to Patterson's office.

When she reached the ship's security office, she could see through the frosted glass that the lights were on so Millie tapped lightly on the door.

There was a muffled response she took for a greeting and quietly opened the door. Not only was Patterson inside, but Donovan Sweeney and Brenda Parcore, whom Millie vaguely recognized.

"Come in Millie." Patterson waved her into the office. "Close the door behind you."

Millie closed the door and made her way to an empty seat next to Donovan.

"I know you're busy with Andy gone so I'll keep this brief." Patterson nodded toward Brenda. "Ms. Parcore claims one of the gallery's expensive limited print paintings is missing and Andy Walker was the last person who viewed it. Do you know anything about this?"

"No." Millie shook her head. "I rarely have an opportunity to visit the art gallery. Andy and I have never discussed art."

"He never mentioned an interest in..." Patterson's voice trailed off as he studied the yellow pad on his desk. "Romare."

Brenda Parcore interrupted. "Romare Tourmine."

"Nope. Never heard of it - him."

The woman gasped. "You're never heard of Romare Tourmine?"

"Uh-uh."

"Ms. Parcore said the last time she saw the painting was when Andy was admiring it. When she arrived this morning to start her shift, the display case was open and the painting was gone."

"Did you ask Andy about it?" Millie asked.

"He's on a plane right now. We won't be able to reach him until at least tomorrow." Donovan turned his attention to the woman. "Have you checked to see if anything else is missing?"

"No. Although I'm going to as soon as I leave here. I've already contacted corporate and informed them of the theft."

"Perhaps you misplaced it," Millie suggested.

The woman's face turned as red as her hair. "I did *not* misplace it. Mr. Walker was admiring the expensive artwork. After he finished looking at it, I placed it back inside the display case and then – poof. It disappeared less than a day later and so did Mr. Walker."

"Andy Walker took an approved leave, Ms. Parcore. You can't go around accusing someone of theft without proof." Millie could tell Patterson had reached his limit with Brenda Parcore's accusations. "We will be investigating the matter, which includes you, as well as contacting the High Seas Gallery offices ourselves."

Brenda straightened her back. "I've already done that. I plan to take a full inventory to make sure there are no other missing artwork pieces." She abruptly stood. "It's apparent you are not going to pursue Mr. Walker's involvement in the missing artwork so I shall conduct my own internal investigation."

The trio watched as Brenda Parcore stomped out of the office, slamming the door behind her.

"That went over well," Millie said. "Maybe she did it. She had opportunity and what better person to pin it on than someone who isn't here to defend himself?"

Patterson leaned back in his chair and ran a hand through his hair. "That's just what we need - a third party company accusing one of our staff members of theft." He turned to Donovan. "Are the Danvers settled into their suite?"

Donovan nodded. "Yes. I received a list of demands...err, requests. It's extensive, especially the one from the missus."

"One of our dancers, Aaron, said he was on another ship when the Danvers entourage cruised with them." Millie was on the fence about mentioning the trouble young Teddy had caused but figured she should throw it out there. "He said Danvers' son, Teddy, is a bit of a troublemaker."

"I heard the same. We'll have to keep an eye on him," Donovan said. "In the meantime, we need to find a volunteer, someone willing to hang out with our young passenger to keep him entertained and out of trouble." He shifted in his chair. "I was thinking one of the younger male entertainers would fit the bill. Do you have any suggestions, Millie?"

"I don't dislike anyone that much," Millie joked. She grew quiet as she mentally reviewed the list of entertainers. "Not right off the top of my head. I'll meet with some of the staff and see if I can rustle up a volunteer." She didn't want to force anyone into the task of babysitting and wanted whoever volunteered to know exactly what they were getting into.

"I'll call a quick meeting and get back with you Donovan." Millie scooched off the edge of the chair and stood. "Is there anything else?"

Patterson nodded toward the door. "Leave the art investigation to us, Millie. You're going to have your hands full this week filling in for Andy, not to mention making sure the Danvers family is entertained and young Danvers stays out of trouble."

"So I guess this is your way of saying Teddy the Terrible is my responsibility?"

"You can handle it, Millie," Donovan replied. "Let me know as soon as you have an escort for the teen."

Millie exited the office and strode down the hall. It was only day one and the Danvers family was already turning the ship upside down.

Chapter 4

Millie waited until the muster drill was over and the ship had cleared the port before assembling the male entertainment staff to discuss the Danvers family.

"Thank you for meeting me on such short notice. I'm sorry to have to call you all here again because I know you're busy, but I need help."

Millie placed both hands behind her back and began to pace. "As we discussed earlier, Mr. Danvers, the CEO of Majestic Cruise Lines, as well as his fiancée, Brigitte, and his son, Teddy, are on board the ship for the week. This was an unexpected surprise and, as you can well imagine, we're scrambling to cover the bases."

She went on to tell them the entire week's activities needed to run flawlessly, that they could not afford glitches in the schedule. "I also have a special request. I need someone who is willing to go above and beyond this week."

"How so?" Kevin eyed her with suspicion.

"I need someone to hang out with Teddy Danvers for the week," Millie blurted out.

The room grew silent.

Millie gazed at the staff. "I can't believe not a single one of you wants such an easy assignment. Think of it, you'll get paid to go ashore, if needed, to play basketball and even video games."

"No way," Kyle said. "Aaron already gave us the heads up. We would be crazy to volunteer."

Millie eyed Aaron.

"I'm sorry Millie. I didn't know you were gonna ask one of us to watch him."

"Well, I am. C'mon guys. I need help," she begged. Despite her best efforts at guilting them into it, cajoling and even bribing, she wasn't able muster up a single volunteer.

"I'm gonna avoid him like the plague," Aaron said. "It's not fair to have one of us play babysitter. Why doesn't Patterson have one of the security guards follow him around?"

"We're here to *entertain* the family, not treat them like criminals." She studied the faces in front of her. "Give me one good reason why you wouldn't want to make sure the Danvers family enjoys their cruise on board Siren of the Seas."

Aaron lifted both hands. "You know my story."

"I like my job," Kevin said.

"Me too," Felix chimed in.

"If no one wants to volunteer, I'm going to be forced to draw straws." Millie waited for a brief moment. "Straws it is." She turned to Danielle.

"I'll go get them." Danielle hurried from the room.

"I understand Aaron's hesitation, but the rest of you? This job will be a piece of cake. Think about it, all you have to do is hang out with one lonely, bored teen." Millie's speech failed to sway the staff and by the time Danielle returned with the straws, she was still without a volunteer.

"Thanks Danielle." Millie took the straws, shuffled them in her hand and held them out to the eight reticent entertainers, minus Aaron whom she'd given a pass because she couldn't blame him.

"Great." Josh Appleton held up the short straw. "I figured I'd get the short end of the stick. Literally."

Josh was new to Siren of the Seas. He'd only been on board as an entertainer for a few weeks. Millie didn't know him very well. He kept to himself and although the other entertainment staff, a tightknit group, tried to include him in non-work related activities, he hadn't seemed interested.

Millie once asked Andy about Josh. According to Andy, the young entertainer had worked for a couple of years on a competitor's cruise line. When the cruise line decided to reposition Josh's ship to Asia for the season, he began looking for another job.

He told Andy during his interview he needed to keep his homeport in Miami, which was the main reason Josh had applied for the position with Siren of the Seas.

Millie patted his arm while the others let out a collective sigh of relief. "It won't be that bad. I promise."

The group shuffled out of the room while Josh hung back. "I have some information on the Danvers family. It includes Teddy's interests, his likes and dislikes; it even listed his one allergy - dust from old books. Avoid the library," Millie said.

Josh chuckled. "That won't be a problem." Despite his obvious dismay for having gotten the short end of the stick, he didn't grumble or complain.

Millie attempted to offer some suggestions on ways to keep the teen busy and out of trouble. She could tell Josh was only half-listening and waved her hand in front of his face. "Earth to Josh. Can you hear me?"

A small smile crossed Josh's face. "Sorry Millie. I was a million miles away." The smile faded.

"You seem preoccupied." Millie shifted in her chair. "I'm a good listener. Would you like to talk?"

Josh started to shake his head and then stopped. His eyes met Millie's and she gave him an encouraging smile. "Whatever you have to say is between us. Sometimes it's good to get it out."

"My mom, she lives in the Miami area. She's been on chemo for a couple months now. I got to spend time with her while our ship was in dry dock."

Millie's heart sank. She grasped Josh's hand. "I'm sorry to hear that. How is she doing?"

"I went with her to her last oncologist visit yesterday. The chemo isn't working. The doctor told us she only has a few months left." Tears filled Josh's eyes and spilled down his cheeks. "Then I had to leave her to come back to work."

Tears burned the back of Millie's eyes. "Oh Josh," she whispered. "I'm so sorry. I had no idea." Guilt over burdening Josh with what now seemed a trite matter, consumed Millie. "I'm going to find someone else to babysit Teddy."

"I-it's okay. Maybe keeping tabs on Teddy will take my mind off Mom."

"Do you have other family? Is there someone at home to care for her?"

"I have a brother who lives in Louisiana. He's on his way to Miami now." Josh swiped at his tear stained cheeks. "I want to be home with her, to take care of her, but I need the money to pay the bills. She can't work. She doesn't have insurance and the only money coming in is what I give her each month."

He sucked in a shaky breath. "There's an experimental drug and a center in Texas willing to take mom for clinical trials but I need at least ten thousand dollars to get her there and pay her expenses for room and board and I don't have it."

"I'm sorry Josh. I wish there was something I could do." Millie silently vowed to give it some thought before she eased the conversation to life on board the ship.

"Millie, do you copy?" Millie's radio began squawking. It was Cat this time.

"Go ahead Cat."

"I wondered if you could swing by for a quick minute."

"I'll head your way shortly." Millie turned her radio down. "Josh, are you sure you want to take on Teddy?"

"I'm sure. How bad can he be?"

Millie had no idea, but she also had an inkling they were going to find out.

Josh and Millie climbed the stairs to deck ten and when they reached the grand suite, Millie knocked on the door but no one answered. "I'll leave a message on their suite phone so we can set up a meeting."

Josh promised he'd check in with her a little later and then Millie headed to *Ocean Treasures*, the onboard gift shop that Millie's friend, Cat, managed.

The store was open for business and busy so Millie wandered around, checking out the new merchandise. She removed a lanyard from the display. Palm trees dotted the fabric strap. Between each palm tree were the words "Siren of the Seas."

"They're nice, huh." Cat stood next to Millie. "Mine has black cats."

"I need a new lanyard, speaking of which, and against my better judgment, I gave Andy's spare access keycard to Danielle. How's business?"

"Brisk." Cat pushed a stray strand of hair from her eyes. "Does the name Brenda Parcore ring a bell?"

"Unfortunately." Millie nodded. "She runs High Seas Gallery, the art auction and gallery one deck down. Why?"

"Brenda was waiting on my doorstep for the store to open. She came in here asking a ton of questions about Andy, did he shop here often, trying to find out what kind of stuff he buys. Then she started asking questions about you."

"Me?"

"Yeah. She mentioned something about some missing art from the art gallery and Andy was the last one to see the art and how she suspected he'd taken the piece."

"What's that got to do with me?"

A group of shoppers made their way inside the store and over to the rack of windbreakers.

Cat lowered her voice. "She said she was sure Andy had taken the expensive artwork and he had an accomplice...you!"

"That's crazy," Millie gasped. "The woman is crazy. She probably took the artwork and now she's trying to pin it on someone else. Andy isn't here to defend himself and I'm so busy trying to fill his shoes, not to mention making sure this week goes off without a hitch, I don't have time to look into it."

Millie's eyes narrowed. "I guess I'll have to make time, now won't I?" Her heart began to race at the thought that not only was Brenda Parcore trying to pin the missing art on Andy, but also her. "I wonder who else she's talked to."

The last thing Millie needed was for Ted Danvers to catch wind there was a theft on board and the art gallery manager was pointing fingers at her.

She'd hoped to butter Danvers up so that Captain Armati and she could ask him about marrying and staying on board the ship. Millie's voice rose an octave as panic set in. "The woman is going to ruin everything."

"Try not to get too stressed out." Cat squeezed Millie's arm. "I'm sure she'll find the artwork and this whole thing will blow over."

Millie hoped that would be the case but she had a bad feeling it was going to be the exact opposite, especially if the woman was telling everyone Millie was somehow involved without a shred of evidence to back up her claim. "She's probably trying to save her own hide."

A customer approached Cat to ask a question.

"Thanks for the heads up." Millie placed the lanyard on the display rack. "I'll get to the bottom of this."

A determined Millie strode out of the store and down the center flight of stairs.

The High Seas Gallery connected two of the specialty restaurants with the lower level of the atrium. On one side was the cigar bar. On the other was the renovated and renamed Coconut's Comedy Club.

Displayed along both sides of the hall were various paintings. Millie had never stopped to admire the artwork and typically hurried from one end of the ship to the other, but not today. She studied several pieces before she found herself in front of the gallery's storeroom.

Through the sheer curtains, she could see someone moving around. Millie grasped the door handle, slid it open and stepped inside.

She spied Brenda Parcore, along with another High Seas Gallery employee Millie vaguely recognized.

Parcore crossed the floor and met Millie near the door. "Yes?"

"I heard that you're making your rounds around the ship, accusing Andy Walker and now me of stealing artwork."

"Artworks," Brenda Parcore corrected. "We've discovered two more missing pieces for a total of three. I guess if you're going to steal, you might as well make it worth your time."

The gallery manager crossed her arms and scowled at Millie. "If you confess now, you might catch a break and get off with a light sentence."

"Confess?" Millie shrieked. "I'm not going to confess. I'm here to tell you to stop spreading false rumors about Andy and me. We did not steal the artwork."

"Oh yeah?" Parcore took a step forward. "I started my preliminary investigation since your cohort, Dave Patterson, refuses to help. I've already uncovered a clue and it points right to you." She jabbed her finger in Millie's direction.

"You're lying," Millie said. "What evidence?"

"I'm not stupid enough to discuss it at this time. You'll have to wait and see."

"I think you lifted the artwork yourself and now you're trying to pin it on someone else," Millie shot back. "And I'm going to prove it."

Millie turned on her heel and marched out of the gallery.

Chapter 5

Millie mentally pushed the investigation aside and descended the stairs to the guest services area. The one person she needed to remain in constant contact with was Donovan. She needed to give him a heads up that she'd found someone to hang out with Teddy.

She squeezed behind the guest service counter and headed for Donovan's office door.

Nikki Tan, one of the guest services employees, hurried over. "You don't want to go in there."

"Why?"

"Because Ted Danvers, a blonde woman and a teenager are inside, meeting with Donovan. The three of them came down here a few moments ago and Donovan looked unhappy. He asked me to call Captain Armati and he's on his way here, too."

Nikki glanced over Millie's shoulder. "There he is now."

Millie took a step back and almost collided with Nic, who placed a light hand on Millie's arm. "Hello Millie."

She took a quick step to the side and the couple locked eyes. "Hello Captain Armati," she said softly. "I heard that you're here to meet with Donovan, but can we talk later?"

"Of course." The corners of Nic's eyes crinkled and his dark smoldering eyes twinkled. "I always have time for you." He shifted his gaze. "I better get in there before old Donovan has a heart attack."

The women watched as the captain rapped lightly on Donovan's office door and then disappeared inside.

Millie glanced at her watch. "I better start making my rounds." She thanked Nikki for giving her a heads up on the Danvers and hurried to the lido deck.

The sail away party was still in full swing and the weather picture perfect as the guests participated in a rousing rendition of "Three Little Birds." She closed her eyes and breathed the salty sea air.

Bright sunshine warmed Millie's face as she hummed along. Yes. Everything would be all right...one way or another.

She darted from the lido deck to the tranquility deck before making a quick pass through the VIP area and then strolling around the mini golf course.

Millie ran into Danielle near the *Hurricane Tiki Bar*. "How's it going?"

"So far, so good," Danielle said. "At least for me it is. That chick who was accusing Andy of stealing the art is interrogating all of the entertainment staff."

"Brenda Parcore?"

"Yeah. Her. She cornered me and asked me how well I knew you. When I told her we were cabin mates, she asked if she could search our cabin."

Millie frowned. "Her latest claim is that Andy was the last person to see the artwork before it went missing and she thinks since he's off the ship, he somehow managed to sneak it off and I'm his accomplice."

"That's ridiculous."

"You didn't let her into our cabin, did you?" Millie could envision Brenda Parcore tearing their cramped cabin apart.

"No. I told her I was certain neither you nor Andy had anything to do with the missing artwork and she was barking up the wrong tree." Danielle smiled as a couple of the bartenders, carrying rainbow-colored tropical drinks, passed by. "She accused me of covering for you and said she wasn't giving up until the culprit or culprits were apprehended."

"She's wasting her time," Millie said. "She probably took it and is trying to pin it on someone else, someone who isn't here to defend himself."

A passenger approached, asking where the nearest restrooms were located. Danielle swept her hand over her head and pointed to the restrooms next to the bar.

The passenger grinned. "Duh."

"Don't worry," Danielle said. "You'll have the ship's layout figured out before you know it."

The women wandered out of the bar area and down the side steps. "Danvers and his entourage met with Captain Armati and Donovan. I'm sure the meeting is over now. I guess I better find out what that was all about."

Danielle wished her luck before telling Millie she was going to run by the sports deck and workout room.

Millie headed to deck seven; past the piano bar and the casino, recently renamed the "Winning

Streak Casino." During the dry dock, workers had installed several new slot machines and rearranged the table games. "Lucky's Bar," one of the busiest bars on the ship, remained unchanged.

A thick cloud of cigarette smoke circled the bar area and Millie picked up the pace as she passed by. There were only a couple of spots on board the ship where smoking was allowed and Lucky's Bar was one of them.

"Millie."

Millie turned to see Donovan coming up behind her. "I've been trying to reach you on the radio."

"Oh?" Millie shifted her gaze and began fiddling with the dial on her radio. "Sorry. I must've accidentally turned it down. I stopped by your office earlier but you were meeting with the Danvers and Captain Armati."

"Let's talk over here." Donovan motioned Millie to follow him to a cushioned bench in front of one of the large ocean view windows.

"Have you found someone to hang out with Teddy?"

"Yes. Josh Appleton, one of the younger entertainment staff, drew the short straw."

"You had to resort to drawing straws?"

"Unfortunately, Teddy has a reputation. Josh and I stopped by the Danvers' suite so I could introduce them to Josh but no one answered."

"That's because they were sitting in my office, going over their list of demands."

"I heard. Annette already has a list of demands, as well."

"So do you." Donovan reached inside his pocket and pulled out several neatly folded sheets of papers. He flipped through the pile. "This one is yours."

Millie took the sheet from Donovan, slipped on her reading glasses and skimmed the list. "Good grief. They have got to be kidding."

"Unfortunately, Danvers isn't kidding. He asked to see a copy of the entire week's entertainment schedule while he was in my office and these are his suggestions."

"Ballroom dancing? We already have line dancing and a samba dance class lined up."

"You'll need to switch it out," Donovan said. "Did you get to the part where Danvers wants golf lessons added?"

"Can we use the mini golf clubs?" Millie joked. The look on Donovan's face told her he was in no mood for jokes. "Sorry."

She resumed her review of the list. "What's this?" Someone had scratched out "art auction" and replaced it with "art appreciation lecture."

"Brigitte wants us to hold an art appreciation lecture. It should be a simple request." Donovan folded the rest of the papers he was holding and shoved them in his pocket.

"Of course," Millie said sarcastically. "All I have to do is find someone who knows how to teach ballroom dancing, a golf instructor not to mention tracking down a set of clubs and then cozy up to Brenda Parcore who, by the way, is convinced Andy and I have something to do with the missing artwork."

"Brenda Parcore is blowing smoke. She doesn't have a leg to stand on. Don't let her intimidate you, Millie."

"I better talk to Patterson, to see if he's made any headway in the missing art investigation," Millie fretted. "The woman is making her rounds around the ship, questioning people who know Andy and me. She even had the nerve to ask Danielle if she could search our cabin."

"She should be the least of your worries. At least Brenda Parcore can't fire you." Donovan stood. "I know you can handle this. Now I need to head up to spa services and go over a few changes with them."

"But she can make my life miserable," Millie muttered under her breath as she watched Donovan head to the bank of elevators.

Millie shifted her attention to the sheet of paper. According to the notes jotted on the side of the schedule, Danvers expected the golf instruction to be offered the following day. Ballroom dancing would take the place of line dancing during the first full sea day. Thankfully, the art appreciation lecture was penciled in closer to the end of the cruise.

Millie unclipped her radio from her belt. "These guys are gonna hate me," she said right before she pressed the talk button. "I need an all entertainment staff meeting backstage in five minutes."

***

Only half of the entertainment staff showed up for the meeting. The rest were out doing their job...entertaining guests at the various onboard events. News of the Danvers' lists of demands had spread among staff and crew like wildfire.

Millie lucked out and discovered one of the female entertainers had once worked as a golf pro while several of the dancers had given ballroom dance classes on other ships.

They agreed to eliminate the line dancing session since it was the one Danvers had scratched out and replaced it with the ballroom dancing. After finalizing the dance class, the women departed, leaving Millie alone with Isla, the ship's new golf instructor.

"I don't have golf clubs."

Millie remembered the time Captain Armati had gone after one of the ship's hijackers with a nine iron. "I...think I know someone who does." Millie tapped her lower lip. "Don't worry about the clubs. I'll make sure there's a set waiting for you inside Andy's office before the day is out."

"Cool." Isla turned to go. "This'll be fun. I haven't swung a club in months."

Millie thanked Isla again and promised she would have the clubs on hand soon. As she walked away, Millie hoped Isla's golf lessons would be good enough for Danvers. If not, it was her head on the chopping block.

She shut off Andy's office light and closed the door. There was only one task left to tackle...chat with Brenda Parcore.

Chapter 6

Millie made it halfway to the art gallery showroom and changed her mind. She needed to think things through first. She needed to approach Brenda in a way that wouldn't appear demanding since, technically, Brenda and the High Seas Gallery staff were not employed by Majestic Cruise Lines.

In other words, Brenda could flat out refuse and there was no way Millie could force her to hold the lecture.

Millie bounced on her tiptoes and peeked into the galley porthole where she caught a glimpse of Annette as she darted around the side of one of the galley prep tables.

She eased the door open and slipped inside. A light *thunk* echoed from the back, near the dessert station and Millie peeked around the corner.

Amit, Annette's right hand man, was piping frosting along the edges of a layered buttercream cake. He nodded and winked at Millie. "Hello Miss Millie."

"Hello Amit." She spied Annette with her head stuck inside one of the floor-to-ceiling refrigerators so she wandered over to inspect Amit's cake. In large letters and scrolled across the front were the words, "Happy Anniversary." Heart-shaped pink and red flowers surrounded the words. "Your cake is beautiful."

"Thank you Miss Millie. I practice every day to create the perfect cake."

"You're doing a great job," Millie said.

"I wondered when you were gonna make an appearance." Annette slipped past Millie to inspect Amit's finished product. "Not bad. This flower looks a little droopy." She pointed at a small imperfection Millie hadn't noticed.

"Ah you're right Miss Annette." Amit's face fell. "I sorry."

"Don't be so hard on yourself, Amit. It's darn near perfect and better than 99% of my other decorating staff." Amit carefully centered the confection in a cardboard box while Millie and Annette wandered to the other side of the galley.

"Andy picked the perfect time to abandon ship," Annette joked. "Have a seat."

"You're not kidding." Millie hopped onto one of the barstools. "Not only is the head of the High Seas Gallery accusing Andy and now me, of stealing artwork, I had to find a babysitter for junior and Donovan just presented me with a list of entertainment schedule changes Danvers wants implemented."

"I've got my own problems." Annette whipped a familiar sheet of paper from her front pocket and handed it to Millie. "Check this out."

Millie slipped her reading glasses on.

"Creamy King Crabmeat Salad Chilled Cucumber Foam & Tuscan Summer Apples."

"Greek Octopus Salad with Basil-Oregano Vinaigrette."

"Lavender-Roasted Duck Breast. (Balsamic Cherries, Chestnut Cappuccino, Salsify and Poached Radish.)"

"Dessert: Affogato Espresso-Flavored Ladyfingers, Layered with Light Mascarpone Cheese & Homemade Vanilla Ice Cream."

She handed the list back. "It looks complicated."

"It is and that's only what the fiancée wants to see on the dinner menu. I haven't even dared look at Mr. Danvers' list. What do they think this is...the Per Maise?"

"Huh?"

"Never mind. It's an expensive restaurant in New York." Annette waved the piece of paper in the air. "I don't have half the ingredients on board to make this stuff and even if I did, I'm not sure our staff would be able to re-create the dishes to her standards."

"And I thought I had problems. All I have to do is swap out a dance instruction class, offer golf lessons, nix the art auction and add an art appreciation lecture."

"I'll trade you."

"No thanks." Millie shook her head. "I could use a little advice on approaching Brenda Parcore about holding the lecture. Remember how I mentioned that a piece of artwork was missing from the High Seas Gallery and she was blaming Andy?"

"Yeah." Annette nodded.

"Now she's blaming me, too," Millie said. "She even had the nerve to ask Danielle if she could search our cabin."

Annette drummed her fingers on the countertop. "I don't doubt it. The woman is a micromanager. Last month, she hosted an art gathering and asked us to supply hors d'oeuvres. Of course, she insisted on a tasting table ahead of time. Picky, picky, picky. You'd think the Queen of England was gonna be there. Anyhoo, I finally had to put my foot down and tell her to take it or leave it."

"Great. Yeah, from my limited interaction with her, I have a feeling she's going to give me a hard time about this lecture." Millie sighed heavily. "I have to do it."

"Or maybe have Danielle ask her," Annette suggested.

"Won't work. Danielle told her in no uncertain terms she wasn't going to search our cabin."

"Donovan?"

"Donovan already has his hands full. He has a whole stack of papers to pass out." Millie hopped off the barstool. "I still need to get with Josh so we can hunt down young Teddy to introduce the two."

"Who is Josh?"

"He's one of the guys in the entertainment staff. Nice kid. Sad story." Millie thought of Josh's mother and his heartbreaking confession she was dying. "I better go."

Millie thanked Annette for letting her vent and told her good luck with the new menu changes before strolling out of the galley.

Despite the few glitches she'd run into since Andy had left, it was nothing compared to losing a loved one. She offered a small prayer for Josh and his mother and made a mental note to ask Josh his mother's name so she could add her to her daily prayer list.

The High Seas Gallery showroom was dark and the gallery empty. Millie made her way down the hall, passing by several large pieces of artwork on display. She reached the end of the hall where she found Brenda Parcore working in front of one of the displays.

She caught Millie's eye and frowned. "You again."

Millie took a deep breath and studied the colorful backdrop of what looked like the Serengeti. Two giraffes craned their necks as they nibbled on the leaves of an odd-looking tree.

Brenda followed her gaze. "That's a baobab tree, found mostly in the Serengeti. I like the contrast between the stark tree and the spectacular sunset. This piece is a Marcelle Volare. It's one of the most expensive pieces we have." She closed the display case cover and turned the lock before dropping a set of keys in her front pocket. "You're not here to admire art."

"No." Millie clasped her hands and the saying, "it's easier to catch more flies with honey than vinegar" ran through her head. "I'm sorry we started off on the wrong foot, Brenda. I'm sure it was extremely distressing to discover that several pieces of art are missing. I'm here to offer my assistance, if there's anything I can do."

"For starters, if you have nothing to hide, you'll let me take a look around your cabin."

Millie ignored the comment. "Again, I apologize for us starting off on the wrong foot. As I'm sure you heard, Mr. Danvers, the CEO of Majestic Cruise Lines, is on board with us this week. He's asked that we replace the art auction with an art appreciation lecture."

Here was Millie's change to lay on the "honey." "It's my understanding that you have a vast knowledge of artwork. I think you would be the perfect person to hold the lecture."

Brenda's eyes narrowed. "I heard Mr. Danvers is on board but this is the first I've heard about an art lecture."

"Since Andy, Mr. Walker, is on leave this week, I'm filling in as cruise director, which leaves me in charge of the ship's activities and the events schedule."

"I see." Brenda paused. "I'll agree to hold an art appreciation lecture if you allow me to search your cabin."

Brenda Parcore had Millie cornered and she knew it. "I..."

"No search, no lecture."

"Okay." Millie relented. "But I'll need some time to clean up my cabin."

"And hide the evidence?" Brenda shook her head. "No way. We go now or it's no deal."

"You can't be serious." This was close to flat out blackmail.

Brenda shrugged nonchalantly. "The choice is all yours and if asked, I'll be sure to tell them how I offered to hold the lecture but you refused to add it to the schedule."

Millie gritted her teeth. "Let's go." She marched down the hall, so ticked off she hoped Brenda had to run to keep up.

When they reached Millie's cabin, she abruptly stopped. "I can't believe I'm doing this." She removed her lanyard from around her neck, slipped her keycard in the door and waited for the faint "click" before twisting the handle and pushing the door open.

Millie fumbled for the light switch, flipped it on and shifted to the side. "Have at it."

Brenda wandered into the neat and tidy cabin. "This is much smaller than mine."

"This isn't a cabin contest."

"Just sayin'." The woman opened the closet doors and peered inside. She shut the doors and ran her hand along Danielle's top bunk before lifting the mattress and inspecting underneath.

She repeated the process with Millie's bunk before moving on to the small dresser where she rummaged through the drawers. Her last stop was the bathroom and she studied the inside for several moments. "You probably already moved the goods," Brenda mumbled.

"What did you say?"

"Nothing."

"That's what I thought. So you agree to hold the art appreciation lecture at four o'clock on Thursday?"

"I didn't say I would do it the same day," Brenda argued.

"That was the deal. Replace the art auction with the art lecture, which is scheduled for four o'clock on Thursday." The woman was starting to get on Millie's last nerve. She didn't have time to play games.

Millie took a menacing step closer.

"Okay. All right. No need to freak out. Four o'clock Thursday. A champagne art lecture. Grimley isn't going to like it though. Art lectures don't bring in the bucks like art auctions. He's already crazy mad about the missing artwork."

Millie hadn't considered that angle. Despite the woman's annoying ways, she didn't want to get anyone into trouble. The woman ultimately was on the hook for the missing artwork, and now she was being pressured into eliminating the art auction in favor of a lecture.

"What if we compromise? You hold the art lecture and I'll take a look at the schedule to see where we can squeeze in an art auction."

"You will?" Brenda was visibly relieved. "Seriously, it would help me out a lot. Grimley is breathing down my neck for an answer on the missing artwork."

A tinge of guilt washed over Millie. The woman was only doing her job. Of course, she was stressed out about the missing artwork, but it wasn't her fault – or Andy's fault, that the artwork was missing. "I'll see where we can squeeze it in."

Millie had left an extra copy of the week's *Cruise Ship Chronicles* on the desk. She pulled the sheets from the pile and scanned the first sheet. "Let's see. Today is Saturday. Tomorrow is San Juan and then we have a sea day. The art appreciation lecture will be late Thursday, the same day we stop in St. Croix."

The women discussed the "at sea" days, which were Monday, Wednesday and Friday. "I can add the art auction to Wednesday's schedule. We'll hold it at the same time we're showing a movie in the theater. You should have a pretty good turnout."

"But that's the day before the lecture," Brenda said. "How about during Monday's sea day?"

Millie studied the schedule. "Okay. I think we can schedule it right after the towel folding demonstration and before the mix master drink mix competition starts."

"Sounds good."

Millie penciled the change on her sheet, grabbed the entire week's schedule and followed Brenda out of the cabin, pulling the door shut behind them.

"I'm sorry I gave you such a hard time about the artwork," Brenda said.

"What about the other staff who work in the art gallery? Have you talked to them?"

"I tried." Brenda wrinkled her nose. "There are only four of us." She rattled off her list of co-workers. "There's Merlin Cuspet. He's worked for High Seas longer than I have. Next is Yasmin. She came from corporate not long ago. Then there's Stanley Zelchon. He's new and currently the one who handles the bidding. All three of them swear they know nothing about the missing artwork."

"Would any of them have access to the prints? Keys maybe or combinations to the safes?"

"Nope." Brenda shook her head. "I'm the only one who has the keys to the frames and the combination to the safe where we store the prints not on display. I never let the keys out of my sight. In fact, I put them under my pillow at night. Andy was the last person with me before the Tourmine print went missing."

"I have my hands full for the time being." Millie thought of Josh and young Teddy Danvers. "Let me get through today and maybe tomorrow I'll have time to look around the showroom and a clue will pop out at me."

"Thanks Millie." The women stopped in front of the theater.

"Time to get back to work." Millie thanked Brenda again and then headed inside. It was time to track down Josh so the two of them could meet with the Danvers family.

When she reached the stairwell, she nearly collided with Josh, who was hurrying down the steps.

"Millie. I'm so glad I found you. We have a problem."

Chapter 7

"Please don't tell me that, Josh. I've had enough problems to last the entire cruise."

"You must've just missed Danielle. She said she ran into Teddy Danvers in the casino."

"Ted Danvers likes to gamble?" He didn't seem the type to Millie, but then she barely knew him.

"No *Teddy* Danvers. The teenager. He was in the casino, playing a nickel slot machines. Felippe, one of the security guards, tried to persuade him to leave. He threatened to have him fired so Danielle stepped in to help and Teddy told her he was going to have her fired, too."

"What happened?"

Josh shrugged. "Finally, one of the security guards called Ted Danvers to the casino and the father escorted his son out of there but not before the senior Danvers reprimanded the entire casino staff for allowing an underage passenger to play."

"Great." Millie ran a hand through her hair. "I hope you can handle him, Josh."

"I don't know if anyone can handle him, but we have to at least give it a try." Josh adjusted his wire-rimmed glasses and cleared his throat. "I'm ready to track down Teddy if you are."

The two of them climbed the stairs, passing through the VIP area as they made their way to the secluded suite section.

"This is it." Millie stopped in front of the grand suite. "Here goes nothing," she whispered under her breath as she rapped on the cabin door.

She heard a small rustling noise before the door abruptly opened and Millie came face-to-face with Ted Danvers.

"Yes. Uh. I'm Millie Sanders, Cruise Director, filling in for Andy Walker." She knew she was babbling but the man was frowning at her and making her nervous. "Josh Appleton, one of our entertainment staff, and I are here to meet your son, Teddy."

The man turned his head. "Teddy!" he bellowed.

A young man with a sullen expression and a crew cut tromped to Danvers' side. "Yeah?"

Before Millie could stop herself, she said the first thing that popped into her head. "Did you win anything in the casino?"

The elder Danvers glared at Millie. "It's inexcusable the ship's staff would allow an underage teenager to play the slot machines. It's not only against company policy, it's illegal."

Teddy rolled his eyes behind his father's back.

"I'm sorry to hear of the unfortunate incident." Millie tugged on Josh's arm. "Josh has offered to show Teddy around the ship and familiarize him with some of the activities."

"Excellent." Ted Danvers propelled his son forward. "I'm sure Teddy appreciates the offer, don't you Teddy?"

"No. I'm perfectly happy hanging out here and playing video games."

"That's no way to spend the week." The senior Danvers gave Teddy another shove. Millie jumped back to avoid colliding with the teen.

"We dress for dinner at six and have dinner reservations at seven." Without waiting for a reply, the door slammed shut and the three of them stood staring at it.

An awkward silence followed.

"Well," Millie finally said. "What would you like to do first Teddy?"

"We can head up to the sports deck," Josh said.

"My knee hurts."

"There's also a mini golf course," Millie piped up.

"Mini golf is for babies."

"What about the arcade?"

Finally, Teddy showed a smidgen of interest. "What kind of games do they have?"

"I don't know. Let's go check it out."

"Millie, do you copy?" It was Danielle.

"You two go on ahead," Millie said. She waited until Josh and Teddy were out of sight.

"Go ahead Danielle."

"The guest services staff is telling me they're waiting for an updated *Cruise Ship Chronicles* schedule. They have to run the copies now or we won't have tomorrow's schedule ready for the second shift housekeeping to drop off in the passenger cabins.

"Oh my gosh. I'll be right there." Millie jogged down the hall, took the steps two at a time and raced across the deck to guest services. "I'm sorry. I forgot all about the revised schedule." She hurried behind the counter, to the computer station in the back.

Millie handed the schedules she was holding to the man behind the desk, before pulling up a chair. The two of them quickly reviewed the entire week's schedule. When Millie was certain the correct changes had been made, she initialed her approval on the draft and waited for a clean copy to print.

With the updated schedule in the works, Millie had enough time to track down Dave Patterson to discuss the missing artwork before starting her late afternoon rounds.

The only events Millie planned to host were the *Welcome Aboard* show that evening, the headliner show, *Gem of the Sea*, later in the week, as well as the past guest party, or as Andy liked to call it the "passenger appreciation party." Last, but not least, she would be responsible for seeing guests off as they exited the ship on port days and greeting them when they returned.

In between, she knew there was at least one mandatory staff meeting.

Millie hurried down the hall. She could see the glow of Patterson's office lights through the frosted glass window. She tapped lightly and quietly pushed the door open.

Patterson was seated behind his desk, scribbling on a yellow pad of paper. "Ah. Millie. I've been wondering how you were doing."

Millie plopped down in an empty chair. "I already feel like I've survived an entire week and this is only the first day," she groaned.

"I heard Danvers and his family have the ship in an uproar."

"They do. One of the entertainment staff has Teddy the Terrible duty. I'm hoping he'll be able to keep an eye on the teenager and keep him out of trouble."

"He needs it. Felippe was in here not long ago. He mentioned something about the young man being up in the casino playing slots. He refused to leave and threatened to have Felippe fired. Security had to call his father down, and he proceeded to lecture everyone on allowing his underage son to gamble."

"Yeah. I think there's a slight amount of family dysfunction going on but who am I to judge?" Millie changed the subject. "I talked to Brenda Parcore about the missing artwork. Have you had a chance to look into the missing paintings?"

"Unfortunately, no." Patterson leaned back in his chair. "Danvers is insisting we post a security guard on the VIP deck to keep an eye on the grand suite so that puts at least one, possibly two of my guys out of commission for the entire week."

"T-that's ridiculous," Millie said. "What exactly does he think is going to happen?"

"Danvers didn't say, only that he wants 24-hour security on the floor." Patterson crossed his arms. "Don't tell me you're already working on figuring out what happened to the artwork."

"The only thing I've done is talk to Parcore and let her search my cabin."

"You did?"

"It's a long story," Millie sighed. "We cut a deal. Back to Brenda. She and I had a nice chat and I think she's afraid she's on the hook for the artwork since she's the only one who has the keys to the displays. She's also the only person who knows the safe combination."

"The missing artwork is her problem, Millie. Since High Seas Gallery is an independent contractor, we have no control over their policies or their employees. In other words, they're on their own."

"Unless High Seas Gallery decides to pursue an investigation and point fingers at Andy or me." Even though Millie believed she'd been able to smooth things over with Brenda, it didn't mean the woman still wasn't going to try to pin it on Millie or Andy, especially after confessing she was the only person who knew the safe combination and possessed the keys to the display frames.

"We have enough to worry about right now."

Patterson was right. They did have enough to worry about, more than enough. Millie slid out of the chair. "So I take it you're not going to bother Andy with this?"

"Nope." Patterson shook his head. "We'll address the missing artwork if, and when, it becomes an issue." He accompanied Millie to the door and opened it. "I heard Danvers is demanding a golf pro / golf lessons. I'm gonna have to check it out myself."

"Thanks for the reminder. I need to track down a set of golf clubs since I don't think the mini golf clubs will pass muster."

"Captain Armati has a nice set of clubs."

"He does and I'm on my way to the bridge now." Millie thanked Patterson for his time and then passed by the bank of elevators as she climbed the stairs to deck ten where both the bridge and Danvers' grand suite were located.

She gave a small wave to the security guard who was standing sentinel at the end of the hall before making her way inside the bridge.

The steady hum of the ship's navigational equipment echoed in the room and she caught the murmur of low voices as she stepped around the corner.

Captain Armati and Staff Captain Antonio Vitale stood on the starboard side of the bridge, their heads close together.

Millie cleared her throat. "Hello Captain Armati, Captain Vitale."

Vitale lifted his head and smiled at Millie. "Captain Armati sounds so formal for a betrothed couple. Don't you want to call him Nic?" he teased.

"Yes, but..."

"I don't mind," Vitale said. "In fact, he lets me call him Nic, too."

"Nic it is." Millie said. "Does this mean I can call you Antonio?"

"Of course." Vitale grabbed a pair of binoculars off the top of the navigational panel and stepped out on the outboard bridge wing for a visual.

Captain Armati waited until the door closed behind him. "My poor Millie. It looks as if you've managed to get saddled with all kinds of extra work this week."

Chapter 8

"It's a mess." Millie was overcome with an overwhelming urge to throw herself in Nic's arms and beg him to have Donovan find someone else to fill Andy's shoes for the week, but she knew he had as much, if not more, on his plate than she did.

"I've had to change the *Cruise Ship Chronicles* to add ballroom dancing, golf lessons and an art lecture. I also recruited one of the entertainment staff to hang out with Teddy, Danvers' son, to try to keep him out of trouble."

"He needs it." Captain Armati glanced outdoors at the staff captain before wrapping his arms around Millie and pulling her close.

She squeezed her eyes shut and placed her head on his chest as she breathed deeply, catching a whiff of his musky cologne. Millie wished she could stay there for the rest of the week.

He reluctantly loosened his grip and took a step back. "I'm afraid we're going to be extra busy this week. I planned to ask you if you wanted to shop for wedding bands in St. Thomas but with Andy gone and Danvers on the ship, we may have to postpone it."

St. Thomas was famous for its jewelry shops and the port featured an expansive shopping area, the Havensight Mall, which was adjacent to the port.

Siren of the Seas was scheduled to change itineraries in a couple of weeks and they would no longer stop in San Juan, St. Thomas and St. Croix. Their new stops would be Saint Martin, St. Kitts and Grand Turk.

Millie had never been to any of the new ports and was looking forward to exploring St. Martin / St. Maarten. The island was divided into two countries. The northern, French side was called

Saint Martin while the southern, Dutch side, was named Sint Maarten or St. Maarten.

Cruise ships docked on the south side, in St. Maarten, and near the town of Philipsburg, which was also famous for its duty-free shopping and jewelry stores galore.

Danielle had visited St. Maarten and mentioned visiting Maho Beach, popular with visitors because of its close proximity to the airport and the fact the inbound planes landed only feet away from the beach area.

Millie wasn't sure she was up for that, but she definitely wanted to check out both the French and Dutch sides of the island and try some local cuisine.

"We can wait until we reach St. Maarten," Millie said as she watched Captain Vitale step back inside and wipe his brow.

"It's a scorcher out there."

"It is," Millie said. "I think I'll pop in and say hello to Scout before I head back to work."

She wandered down the narrow hall, and after entering the four-digit code, Millie opened the captain's apartment door and began calling the Yorkshire terrier's name. "Scout?"

Millie thought she heard a small whimper and quickly realized something was wrong with Scout. She slammed the apartment door shut and ran down the hall.

"Scout?" Millie's panicked voice raised an octave. "Where are you?" Her eyes darted around the living room.

A small movement near the balcony blinds caught her attention. Scout was tangled in the blinds' cords. "Oh my gosh."

Millie raced to the other side of the room and fell to her knees. She fumbled with the strings as she frantically worked to remove a section of the cord from Scout's front right paw.

"Hold still," she soothed.

After untangling the cords and freeing Scout, Millie ran her hand along his legs. "How on earth did you manage to get wrapped up in the cords?"

When Millie finished her quick examination, she scooped him into her arms and held him close. "Let's get some water and a snack."

She carried the small dog to the kitchen and gently placed him on the floor before filling his food and water dishes.

While Scout ate, Millie returned to the living room. After inspecting the cords, she stepped back inside the tidy kitchen and began rifling through the drawers where she found a package of unopened shoestrings. "Perfect."

Millie deftly banded the cords together and tied them so that they were out of Scout's reach.

When she finished, Millie stood back to admire her handiwork while Scout promptly pounced on her shoe and began pawing at her leg.

"You shouldn't have another treacherous tangle with the cords." She lifted the small dog and held him close as he licked the side of her chin and lunged forward in an attempt to nibble on her earring. "You scared me half to death," she scolded.

"I'll take you out for a quick break and then I have to get back to work." Millie followed Scout out onto the balcony for a brief potty break and after reassuring herself he was all right, she made her way to the front door.

Millie returned to the bridge where she discovered First Officer Craig McMasters had joined the other captains.

She pulled Nic off to the side and told him about Scout's predicament and how she'd secured the cords.

"He's never done that before." Captain Armati frowned. "Poor Scout. I wonder how long he was tangled up."

"I don't know." Millie reassured him Scout had recovered and after a quick good-bye to the other men inside the bridge, she headed to the outer corridor before remembering she needed to borrow Nic's golf clubs.

She stepped back inside. "I need to borrow your clubs for the golf lessons."

"They're in the closet." Captain Armati walked over to the wall of closets, reached inside a center cabinet and pulled out a set of clubs. "My Callaway clubs are like new."

"I'll make sure Isla takes good care of them," Millie promised. She thanked him for the loan, shifted the bag to her shoulder and carried them out of the bridge. It was time to check on Teddy and Josh.

She suspected if Teddy had a penchant for bright, noisy machines, that he and Josh might be inside the video arcade.

Millie's hunch was correct and she found the two of them playing a virtual hunting game. She crept up behind them and silently watched them play.

"You gotta follow the target," Teddy told Josh. "See? Don't take your eyes off it." The animated bear stumbled forward, fell to the ground and closed his eyes.

"Great shot," Millie complimented.

Josh turned. "Millie."

"Hi Josh." She nodded at Teddy. "How's it going?"

"Great. Teddy and I toured the Teen Scene and there wasn't much happening so we stopped by *Waves* to grab some pizza and now we're here."

"We're gonna head to the exercise room next and pump some iron." Josh pushed his shirtsleeve up and flexed his muscles.

"Then I'm gonna kick his butt at basketball." Teddy dropped the plastic rifle in the holder and limped across the arcade, dragging his right foot as he walked.

"Did..." Millie started to ask Teddy if he'd hurt his foot when she noticed a metal strap attached to his shoe.

Millie caught Josh's eye and he gave her a small shake of the head. "Sounds like you two have the rest of your day planned out."

"I'm gonna check out the asteroids game." Teddy limped across the arcade, slipped his keycard in the slot and reached for the controls.

Millie motioned Josh to the back of the arcade. "Teddy's leg."

"Yeah." Josh nodded. "I haven't asked about it, but judging by the way he walks and a couple of the comments he's made, the brace is a permanent fixture. He also made a comment that he thinks Brigitte and Danvers are happy to have him out of their hair."

"How sad," Millie said. "Maybe that is the reason why he's always acting up. Teddy is looking for attention, good or bad." Millie had been quick to judge him based on what she'd heard. She remembered one of her favorite sayings, "Before you judge a man, walk a mile in his shoes."

"I feel guilty," Millie said.

"Me too. I was thinking the same thing," Josh said. "I have to take him back to his cabin soon."

"Hey Josh." Teddy waved him over to the game. "Check out my score."

"I better get going." Millie thanked Josh again and slowly walked out of the arcade, vowing that once the Danvers family was off the ship, she was going to find a way to reward Josh. Maybe she could talk to Andy about giving him the entire day off the next time they docked in Miami.

She lugged the clubs to Andy's office and set them near the door. Millie had time to visit the crew mess to grab a bite to eat before heading back stage to prepare for the first Welcome Aboard show.

The ship's main dining room had just opened for first seating, which was when the housekeeping staff started their second shift and turn down service.

The early evening hours were also a busy time for the wait staff and servers, not to mention the kitchen crew. The following day, Sunday, would be a little less stressful since it was a port day in San Juan. It would give Millie a chance to catch her breath.

She wondered if Josh would volunteer to accompany the Danvers on shore or if the family was even getting off the ship in port. She hoped they would.

Millie eased a spoonful of black beans and rice onto the side of her plate. She added a slab of bar-b-cue pork ribs, a rare treat for the crew, as well as a scoop of mashed potatoes and a small piece of corn on the cob before making her way to a table near the door.

She bowed her head and prayed over her food, adding a special prayer for Teddy and Josh.

"There you are," Donovan Sweeney's voice echoed in her ear.

"Oh no." Millie lifted her head. "Now what did I do?"

"Nothing." Donovan settled into the chair across from her. "I just left Patterson's office and was walking by when I saw you so I thought I would check in."

"Everything is under control," Millie reported. "A couple of the dancers have taught ballroom dancing before so I have that covered. I dropped the line dancing. I also found out one of our female dancers is a former golf pro so I scheduled her for the golf lessons and borrowed Captain Armati's golf clubs."

Millie told him she was able to convince Brenda Parcore to offer an art appreciation lecture. She left out the part where she relented and let the woman search her cabin.

"How is young Teddy doing? I heard he was caught gambling in the casino and threatened to have one of the security guards and Danielle fired."

"Yeah. Can you believe it?" Millie pinched the ends of the spareribs and nibbled the edge, careful to keep the sauce away from her white blouse. "You should try the ribs. The sauce starts out sweet but by the time you swallow, there's a little kick to it."

"They look good. I think I will." Millie watched as Donovan made his way to the empty buffet where he grabbed a small plate and filled it with ribs before returning to his seat.

"I just left Josh Appleton and Teddy. They were playing video games in the arcade."

Donovan nodded and picked up one of the ribs. "Last I heard the family is getting off the ship in San Juan for the day. They have reservations in the specialty restaurants each night except for Friday's formal night where they're dining at the captain's table."

Millie wondered if she would be invited to the captain's table. If so, it would give Nic and her a chance to approach Danvers about allowing them to wed and stay on board the ship together.

"Ah." Donovan waved his sparerib in Millie's direction. "I can see the wheels turning. Friday's meal might be the perfect opportunity to approach Danvers about your upcoming nuptials. I'll finish getting the crew signatures on the petition and Captain Armati can present it to him during dessert."

"Are you going to dine with them?" Millie asked. Typically, the ship's captain, the cruise director, occasionally the assistant cruise director and the executive chef, if he or she was available, were invited to the dinner as well as several passengers.

Although passengers were randomly selected and invited to dine at the captain's table, loyal past guests or celebrity guests had better odds of being invited.

"Yes. Since Andy is on leave, you'll be invited, too. I offered to join you to hopefully head off any of Danvers' concerns during the dinner."

Donovan and Millie finished their food and she glanced at her watch. "I need to head backstage for a brief meeting with the staff before the *Welcome Aboard* show starts." The pair emptied their scraps in the recycle bin and placed their dirty dishes in the tray on their way out.

The *Welcome Aboard* show had not changed since Millie began working on the Siren of the Seas. It was a variety show and highlighted the assorted entertainment featured during the weeklong cruise. It included a couple of Vegas-style dance numbers, ten minutes of the comedian's family-friendly act as well as a few magic tricks by their magician, Julio Marchan.

Since Andy handled the headliner shows, Millie didn't know Marchan well. He popped on and off the ship, depending on the ship's itinerary. Andy told her he split his time between their ship and two others in the fleet...the Baroness of the Seas and the Marquise of the Seas.

Thankfully, the staff had performed the *Welcome Aboard* show so many times; Millie was certain they could do it with their eyes closed.

There were no last minute issues and Millie freshened up before taking the stage to open the show.

Her eyes were drawn to the VIP area in the front, the seats reserved for the Danvers' family. The seats were empty and Millie let out a sigh of relief.

"Thank you for joining us this evening for our *Welcome Aboard* show. Tonight we'll give you a taste of our ship's entertainment, from our comedian to our magician and of course, Siren of the Seas' spectacular singers and dancers."

Millie thought about skipping Andy's favorite joke, but decided to go ahead with it. "I'm sure by now you've checked out your cabin and hopefully your luggage showed up."

She lifted her hand. "By a show of hands, how many of you have used the toilet in your cabin?" Millie smiled as almost everyone raised his or her hand. "Our chief engineers have completed an extensive study of the vacuum system and discovered if we all flush our toilets at 8:15 this evening, we'll be on track to reach San Juan within two hours."

The joke got a good number of chuckles. The ship's toilets ran on a vacuum system and the first time she'd ever tried it out, the suction noise had startled her.

At least once since she'd joined Siren of the Seas, an entire section of the ship's toilets had stopped working. It took the maintenance crew several hours to conclude that one of the guests had attempted to flush disposable baby diapers down the delicate system.

Millie wrapped up her speech by introducing the Siren of the Seas dance crew and then quickly exited stage right. She stood behind the curtain to watch. It never ceased to amaze her how the dancers managed to make it look so easy, all the while, the ship was moving, not to mention the stage wasn't much bigger than a postage stamp.

She gave them all a thumbs-up after their number ended and then returned to the center of the stage to introduce the comedian. The rest of the show went off without a hitch. The second show was identical to the first and after it ended, she let out the breath she'd been holding.

Millie had survived her first headliner show without Andy.

"Fantastic job," Danielle hurried over. "I caught the second part of the show and you're like the female version of Andy," she joked.

"Thanks. I think." Millie smiled. "I'm exhausted. I still have to run up to the lido deck before taking a short break and then head back upstairs for the late night festivities." The schedule was grueling and it would be a long workweek with little time for sleep.

Millie finished helping the dancers put their costumes away and inventoried the closet before locking the door and slowly making her way out of the theater.

She found Dave Patterson seated on the stairs next to the theater doors. "Hello Millie."

Millie could tell from the expression on Patterson's face that something was wrong.

"I just met with Brenda Parcore. Another piece of art has gone missing and she insists you were admiring it right before it vanished."

Chapter 9

"You're kidding," Millie said. "I'm beginning to think this woman is trying to frame me." She thought of the surveillance cameras all over the ship. "All you have to do is check out the video surveillance and you'll see I wasn't anywhere near there, other than when I talked to Brenda earlier about hosting an art lecture."

"I've already reviewed the video. Unfortunately, Brenda moved the piece in question inside the showroom where we have no footage."

"The door wasn't locked?"

Patterson shrugged. "Ms. Parcore told me they don't lock the showroom floor since all of the pieces are either locked in the safe or locked in the display cases. Since the gallery rents the showroom space, it's their responsibility to install cameras."

"So there are no cameras," Millie said. "Meanwhile, someone walked inside the showroom, removed a painting, slipped it under their shirt and then walked out."

"Possibly. There is one common thread so far. All of the missing pieces are small and none is larger than a 5"x7" frame. I noted several passengers we caught on video walking by. Suharto is working to track them down now so we can talk to them."

"I guess that lets Andy off the hook," Millie said. "I think Parcore is stealing the artwork and trying to pin it on me." The woman had opportunity. She was the only one with a key to the cases. "How could I have taken the painting? I don't have a key and she does."

"We're also investigating Ms. Parcore, but in the meantime, we still have to question all possible suspects."

"And I'm a suspect," Millie rubbed her brow. "I can't believe she's throwing me under the bus."

"Brenda is cooperating and has agreed to let us search the gallery and inspect the artwork outside the gallery under her direct supervision, of course."

"Of course. Did she mention I already let her search my cabin?"

"Yes." Patterson frowned. "You did, but I guess it didn't eliminate her suspicions."

He continued. "Don't stress out over it tonight, Millie."

"That's easier said than done."

Dave Patterson promised he would keep Millie in the loop if they uncovered additional information.

Millie thanked him and then headed up to the lido deck. She swung by the beverage station for a cup of black coffee and then made her rounds, cruising by the piano bar, the atrium bar and the Winning Streak Casino.

She slowed as she neared *Ocean Treasure*. The gift shop was holding its "inch of gold" sale and passengers flocked around the tables lining the corridor. She caught Cat's eye, gave her friend a quick wave and kept moving.

Millie had planned to return to her cabin to rest, but instead decided she needed to start her own investigation into the High Seas heist and the gallery staff.

She was certain Donovan kept his own set of files on the company and the staff who worked on board the Siren of the Seas. She also knew there was no way Donovan would let her see the files.

Millie's only other option was to research the company online so she headed to the crew's shared computers. She wandered into the empty room, settled into a station near the door and logged on using her access code.

She typed in "High Seas Gallery." The home page displayed a list of the company's top executives. Millie briefly read Jim Grimley's bio. Grimley was the manager of shipboard operations and Millie recalled Brenda specifically mentioning Grimley's name. Nothing in his biography stuck out as a possible clue.

She scrolled the screen when another name caught her eye. Christy Parcore. The brief bio stated Christy was High Seas' human resources director. Originally from California, Parcore currently resided in Miami.

Millie wiggled the mouse. "I wonder if Christy Parcore and Brenda Parcore are related." It was an uncommon name. What if the two women had cooked up a scheme to steal artwork from the gallery?

She opened a second screen and typed in "Brenda Parcore, Miami, Florida." When an address in Miami Gardens popped up, Millie knew she was onto something.

It made perfect sense. Christy helped Brenda land the cushy job on board the Siren of the Seas. Brenda admitted she was the only one with the code to the safe and the only one who had keys to the display cases.

Millie scooted her chair to the phone on the wall and dialed Donovan's extension.

"Hello?"

"Hi Donovan. It's Millie. I have a quick question."

"Does it involve Danvers? If it does, I don't want to hear it."

Millie chuckled. "No. It involves High Seas Gallery. I was wondering how long Brenda Parcore, the manager, has worked on board our ship."

"Don't tell me you're poking your nose in Patterson's investigation."

"I'm not poking my nose in Patterson's investigation," Millie said. "It's a simple question."

Millie listened to the sound of rustling papers. "She's been on board for about four months."

"Not very long," Millie said. "Thanks Donovan." She started to hang up. "Wait. One more question."

"No you can't see their files," Donovan said.

"I know I can't. I wasn't even gonna ask. Brenda Parcore told me there were three other gallery employees on board the ship. Would it be against company policy to tell me how long they've been on Siren of the Seas?"

"I guess not. I mean it's public information." She heard papers rustling again.

"Merlin Cuspet has been on board for two years. Yasmin Odo, for a little less than a year and Stanley Zelchon's first day was Friday."

"That's interesting," Millie said as she grabbed a pad of paper and pen from the corner of the computer desk. "Can you spell the names for me?"

Donovan spelled the names. "You need to let Patterson handle this."

"I would except for the fact that Parcore is blaming me for the missing artwork," Millie said. She thanked Donovan for the information and said good-bye before turning her attention to the computer screen.

She found nothing on Yasmin Odo. Merlin Cuspet had worked for one of High Seas competitors, according to the brief article she was able to find.

Stanley Zelchon had been a fine art auctioneer for a large, global company. Millie wondered why on earth he'd gone from being a high-end, prestigious art auctioneer who probably made boatloads of money selling expensive art, to working in an art gallery on board a cruise ship.

Millie scribbled a star next to Zelchon and Parcore's names, making them her number one and number two suspects. Parcore, because she was the only one with access to the artwork and Zelchon because he left a prestigious job and it didn't add up.

She exited the search screens and shut the computer off before heading back upstairs to begin her final rounds. The atrium's violinist was gone and *Killer Karaoke* was under way.

The piano bar was still packed and now standing room only. Millie made a mental note to mention it to Andy. Perhaps it was time to move the piano bar to a larger venue on board the ship.

The Tahitian Nights Dance Club was also bustling. Her last stop before heading to her cabin was the lido deck. It was the red-hot 70's dance party and guests crowded the dance floor.

When she reached her cabin, Danielle was already inside and in the bathroom. Millie would have loved to switch her radio off but with Andy gone, she was on call 24-hours so she plugged it into the charger before turning it up and kicking off her work shoes.

Danielle popped out of the bathroom. "Hey Millie. You look as tired as I feel."

Millie lifted both hands above her head. "I'm whupped. I'm sorry but I'm leaving my radio on in case of an emergency and I have to be up at five for the sunrise stride." She stifled a yawn, grabbed her pajamas and headed into the bathroom.

When she emerged, the cabin lights were already off. Millie could hear Danielle's soft snores coming from the top bunk so Millie dropped her dirty clothes on the floor next to her bunk and crawled into bed.

Although she was exhausted, her mind refused to shut down. She thought of Josh Appleton and his mother's cancer. Millie thought of young Teddy Danvers and his leg brace. She also thought of Andy. She hoped he'd made it home safely and was spending precious time with his mother.

Millie prayed for all of them and added a prayer for her own family and for Nic, and thanked God they were all healthy. She also prayed for a peaceful, stress-free week and that everything would go off without a hitch.

After finishing her prayers and right before Millie drifted off to sleep, she thought about Brenda Parcore and the missing artwork. Despite everything Millie had on her plate, she needed to clear both Andy's name and hers. But how?

Chapter 10

Millie tossed and turned as she thought about the artwork. Patterson mentioned that the stolen pieces were small. Even if they were small, it wasn't as if the thief or thieves could fold the artwork up and shove it in their suitcase. It would have to be carefully stored, carefully packed.

The next morning, Millie sprang from bed, ready to get her first full day as cruise director under way. She sailed through the sunrise stride workout, swung by the beverage station for her first cup of coffee and then headed down to Patterson's office to meet with him and his staff to discuss the San Juan port stop.

Earlier, before Millie crawled out of bed, she felt the familiar shudder as the ship docked. Judging by the chatter on the radio, the ship still hadn't cleared customs and when she reached

Patterson's office, she discovered there was a minor problem.

One of the passengers, a non-US citizen, was experiencing chest pains and they were attempting to expedite the ship's clearance so they could get her into an ambulance, which was waiting near the gangway.

Thankfully, the ship finally cleared and the passenger and her family were the first to be escorted off.

Millie hurried to the gangway to see the rest of the passengers off.

Danielle joined her moments later. "Has Danvers and entourage departed?"

"No. Last I heard they were going to get off the ship and tour Castillo San Cristóbal. I'm hoping I'll have time to chat with their personal assistant, to make sure everything is running smoothly on their end." Millie had heard the name of the person assigned to assist the Danvers family but she couldn't place the face.

In between bursts of passengers disembarking for the day, Millie filled Danielle in on the latest missing art.

"Has Patterson searched the gallery yet?"

"I don't know." Millie shared her theory, how it was possible the artwork was still on board the ship, hidden by whoever heisted it. "It has to be the same person."

"They have a lot of nerve to steal it right off the ship," Danielle said. "What about the ship's surveillance cameras? If the last piece of art was on display inside one of the cases, wouldn't someone have noticed it?"

"It was on display *inside* the gallery and our video surveillance is only set up to record the hallway out front. The gallery rents the showroom space and it's their responsibility to install cameras, which they haven't done."

Millie thought of Brenda Parcore and the mysterious Christy Parcore. Perhaps the two had concocted a scheme to steal the artwork. Brenda, not to mention all of the other gallery employees, would know there were no cameras inside the gallery.

The fact Millie had viewed the piece of artwork shortly before it was stolen and the same thing had happened to Andy was suspect. It also placed Brenda Parcore at the top of Millie's list of suspects.

A young family approached to ask if it was safe to venture out on their own instead of taking one of the ship's recommended excursions. The majority of the ship's recommended excursions were pricey and Millie knew firsthand that guests could purchase cheaper excursions with a better selection on their own.

She thought of her first ever excursion in Jamaica with Annette, where a local had tried to rob them. When Annette fought back, it was Millie's first inkling there was more to Annette than met the eye.

Millie would never recommend passengers venture out on their own in Jamaica, although many of them did.

She'd heard a rumor that a few years back a group of cruise ship passengers had been robbed at gunpoint during a tour of the rain forest. "I wouldn't venture too far out without a guide. Personally speaking, it's an easy walk to the fort and Old San Juan if you're interested in shopping or having lunch." The couple thanked Millie for the tip and made their way off the ship.

Danielle watched them depart. "I'm always leery of recommending people venture out on their own."

"I am too," Millie said. "That's why I go by the 'bubble rule.'"

"Bubble rule?"

"If there's a guard and a gate surrounding the ship's docking area, I call it the bubble zone and suspect there have been crimes committed near the port. If there are no chain link fences and/or guards, aka the bubble areas, then I'm guessing there isn't a serious crime problem, of course, you should never let your guard down."

"Ah. I never thought of that," Danielle said. "The bubble rule. I like it."

"I've never shared my suspicions with passengers since I have no proof. Maybe I'm just being paranoid."

"I don't think so."

A flurry of activity near the bank of elevators caught Millie's eye. Ted Danvers, Brigitte, young Teddy and Josh, strolled toward them.

Millie smiled brightly. "I heard you're touring the old fort today."

Brigitte wrinkled her nose. "I don't see why in the world we're visiting a stinky, dirty, moldy old fort."

"History," Ted said. "It won't hurt you, Brigitte. After we're done, we'll visit the shopping district."

Brigitte mumbled something under her breath and lifted her chin. "I see you added my suggestion for ballroom dancing lessons to the schedule. I do hope you have competent staff, trained to instruct the class."

"Yes." Millie nodded. "You won't be disappointed." At least, Millie hoped she wouldn't be disappointed.

Brigitte patted Teddy's arm. "Teddy has a brilliant suggestion. He thinks you should have a table tennis contest."

"That is a good idea," Millie agreed. She didn't tell them they had removed the table tennis contest from the schedule a few weeks earlier due to lack of interest, and replaced it with a cupcake-decorating contest.

Andy considered the swap a huge success since it was a family-friendly event, not to mention the ship charged an admission fee to cover the cost of supplies, with a little extra "padding," of course.

"Josh and I are gonna ride Segways," Teddy told Millie.

"Now that sounds like fun," Millie said. "Don't forget to be back on board the ship by four." She told them good-bye and Teddy led the way off the ship, his limp still visible but not nearly as noticeable as the previous day.

"It looks as if Josh is doing a great job of keeping young Teddy out of trouble."

"Yes. I'm glad he drew the short straw."

Danielle and Millie spent the next hour chatting with guests, answering questions and reminding them to be back on board the ship by four.

After the crowds thinned, Danielle offered to host the cartoon trivia contest on deck seven.

Despite Millie's original concerns about Danielle, she was turning out to be the perfect assistant. "Thanks Danielle. I appreciate all of your help."

"You're welcome." Danielle waved Andy's extra keycard in front of her face. "I would like to point out that I haven't gotten into trouble, at least not yet."

"And you better not." Millie wagged her finger at Danielle before the young woman headed to the bank of elevators.

Millie made her way down the stairs to Dave Patterson's office. It was time to find out if he'd had a chance to search the gallery and to share her suspicions with him.

Tracking Patterson down turned out to be tricky. Millie finally gave up and resorted to radioing him instead. Oscar, Patterson's right hand man, answered the call, telling her Patterson was in a meeting.

Millie suspected he might be meeting with Brenda Parcore so she made her way to the art gallery. The gallery was dark and she stuck her head inside the empty room.

"Can I help you?" A male voice echoed in Millie's ear. She clutched her chest and jumped back.

"Oh. N-no. I was uh, looking for Dave Patterson," she stuttered.

"Head of security?" The man's eyes traveled to Millie's nametag. "Ah. Millie Sanders. You're Brenda Parcore's new friend."

"I...wouldn't call us friends."

The man smiled, showing off a sparkling set of pearly whites. "It was a joke."

The man looked familiar. Millie glanced at his nametag, *Stanley Zelchon*. He was the man she'd read about on High Seas Gallery's website the previous day. "Mr. Zelchon. I know Mr. Patterson is investigating the artwork thefts and he planned to take a look around the gallery. I thought maybe I would find him here."

"You just missed him and Ms. Parcore." The man shoved his hands in his pants pockets and rocked back on his heels.

Millie was curious to know what Zelchon thought. "What's your take? I mean, I'm guessing you've worked as an art dealer for several years. Have you ever run across thefts like this?"

Zelchon's eyes narrowed and he quickly resumed his poker face. "The missing artworks are easily worth several thousand dollars each. Only a fool would try to hide them in a suitcase or by other means. The pieces need to handled carefully or risk damaging the goods, therefore making the theft a total waste of time."

"I'm not familiar with high end art," Millie said. "How would someone pack the pieces to avoid damage?"

"That's a good question. Are you thinking of transporting a valuable piece of art?" The way Zelchon posed the question caused Millie to wonder if he thought she was asking because she was planning on packing a piece of art – a piece of stolen art.

"No. I was trying to figure out if, and how, someone managed to get the artwork off the ship."

Zelchon placed his forefinger on the bridge of his glasses. "They would need to anticipate the conditions in which the artwork would be transported, something of utmost importance. One must take into consideration humidity and environmental conditions. High Seas Gallery uses special packing crates. We line the box or crate with insulation paper, polyethylene, or bubble wrap to create a moisture and thermal barrier."

Zelchon droned on about protecting the artwork using soft materials to sandwich between and making sure the person who packaged the art wore white cotton gloves to prevent unwanted fingerprints or dirt. "All materials must be acid free since certain acids could drastically alter the artwork's condition."

Millie interrupted. "So you're saying if the person or persons who stole the art were knowledgeable and let's go with the assumption that they are, it's almost impossible the artwork left this ship without someone noticing?"

"Yes. If they were knowledgeable in handling art," Zelchon agreed. "The fact they specifically targeted some of the smaller, more valuable pieces leads me to believe that's the case. There's no way they could have walked off the ship with special packing materials."

Millie tilted her head thoughtfully. That left only two possibilities...the artwork was still somewhere on board the ship, or the thieves had found a creative way to get the goods off and Millie knew the perfect person who might be able to shed some light on her theories.

Chapter 11

Annette Delacroix shifted the rim of her crisp white chef's hat and swiped her bangs from her eyes. "Are you sure it's going to be worth our time to bribe Sharky? Isn't he a maintenance supervisor?"

"He is," Millie said. "But he also spends a great deal of time supervising the workers who offload the ship. Say someone attempted to smuggle several valuable pieces of art off the ship. Stanley Zelchon explained how they would need to be packaged in a particular manner. If it was an inside job, it's possible the person or persons might attempt to funnel it through the loading docks."

"True. I guess it wouldn't hurt to give it a try. Nothing ventured, nothing gained."

"And even if the missing pieces are still on board, whoever stole them will eventually try to get them off. We can ask Sharky and his men to keep an eye out for them," Millie said. "If you're willing to help me out, I'll run down to his office to see if we can hammer out a mutually beneficial agreement."

Millie first met Sherman Kiveski, aka "Sharky," not long ago, after he assisted Millie, Annette and Cat in an investigation involving an attack on Brody, Millie's friend.

Sharky had agreed to loan the women maintenance crew uniforms so they could work undercover to keep an eye on Brody in exchange for a made-to-order, gourmet dinner.

Since helping them, the daytime supervisor had contacted Millie once, asking if she needed assistance in exchange for another meal. She hadn't needed help, until now.

"Would you like me to go with you?" Annette didn't wait for an answer. "Amit."

"Yes Miss Annette." Amit hurried over.

Millie took one look at Amit's face and began to laugh. It was covered in a thin layer of cocoa-colored brown powder, a sharp contrast to the whites of his eyes. "What in the world?"

Annette placed a fisted hand on her hip. "Amit, you look like you dunked your head in a can of cocoa powder." She swiped her index finger across Amit's cheek and licked the tip. "Yes, I do believe it is cocoa powder."

"Oh no. I put the cocoa powder in the large mixing bowl and turn it on. It go 'poof' and explode in my face." Amit grabbed the bottom of his apron and attempted to clean his face, which only made matters worse.

"Hang on." Annette grabbed a kitchen towel from the drawer, hurried over to the sink to dampen it and then returned to wipe Amit's streaked face. "I've told you a million times, you have to start out on low speed. You can't turn it on high."

"I know, Miss Annette, but I got distracted."

"What were you making?" Millie asked.

"Miss Annette's chocolate melting cake."

"I don't put cocoa powder in my chocolate melting cake," Annette said.

"You don't?" The whites of Amit's eyes widened.

"No."

Millie started to chuckle and quickly dissolved into a fit of laughter. "Poor Amit." She clutched her stomach.

"Poor Amit? Poor me." Annette turned the dishrag over and finished wiping Amit's face. "I appreciate you trying to help, Amit, but next time, if you're in doubt, ask me for the recipe." She tapped the side of her forehead with her finger. "All of my recipes are up here."

"A mind like a steel trap," Millie teased.

Annette shot her a dark look.

"Sorry." Now was not the time to get on Annette's bad side.

"Millie and I need to take care of something downstairs so I'm going to leave you in charge. I'll be back in half an hour or less and then we can start prepping for the afternoon tea." She untied her apron and hung it on the hook near the door before easing her hat off and placing it on top. "Stay away from the mixer."

Millie winked at Amit and he grinned at her while Annette's back was turned.

"At least he tries."

"I know." Annette held the door for Millie. "And he's a fast learner but there are times when I feel like we take three steps forward and two steps back."

Millie hadn't ventured down to deck zero, the maintenance department and cargo area of the ship, since her undercover operation during the recent dry dock. This was the area where all of the ship's food, not to mention supplies and passengers' luggage were loaded and unloaded.

When the women reached the lower deck, they passed by the "Go Green" door, where all of the ship's leftover food and scraps were pureed and then released into the ocean as fish food.

They turned right and started down a narrow corridor before reaching Sharky's office. Annette twisted the doorknob. "It's locked."

"Watch out." Millie pressed her back against the wall to avoid colliding with workers who were pushing a cart filled with boxes of bananas. "We're looking for Sharky."

The workers paused. "You just missed him. He's back by the bay, near the zone five unloading area. Take this out to the main corridor, turn left and go straight. You'll run right into it."

Millie thanked the workers for the information. The women retraced their steps to the main corridor and strolled down the hall.

Annette eyed the dimly lit overhead pipes as they walked. "This place is the stuff nightmares are made of."

"You'd think they would put brighter lighting down here. It's kind of creepy." Millie shivered. She thought about Francisco Garcia, the maintenance worker who'd been murdered not long ago.

The beep of a forklift echoed in the hall and grew louder.

"Stand back." Annette grabbed Millie's arm as she jumped to the side and pulled her friend with her. The forklift driver nearly sideswiped them.

"Watch where you're going!" Annette shouted.

The forklift never slowed.

"Jerk," Millie said. "We oughta report him."

The women moved cautiously as they continued down the hall, and when Millie caught a whiff of cigar smoke, she knew they were getting close.

"It's like an obstacle course down here." Annette stuck her head around a stack of wooden pallets. "I see him."

Sharky was sitting on his black scooter, chewing on the end of a lit cigar. He began waving his hands at two workers. "I already explained to you numbskulls – we can't store the cases of bleach and bottles of vodka in the same area."

"But…" One of the workers unwisely decided to test Sharky's patience.

"What part of no don't you understand?" Sharky shot out of his seat, balancing his 4'10" frame on the scooter's footrest. "Store the bleach in storage room seven and lock the vodka in storage room two." He sank onto the seat. "And I'll be inventorying the goods to make sure all the booze is accounted for."

One of the men mumbled under his breath.

Sharky cupped his hand to his ear and leaned forward. "What's that? You want me to move you to recycling so you can sort cans and bottles?"

"No."

"That's what I thought. Now get back to work."

The men hurried down the hall and Annette took a step forward. "Sounds like you run a tight ship down here. I admire that."

"I didn't know I had an audience." Sharky shifted to the side and lifted a brow. "Ah...two of my favorite gals. This must be my lucky day. Let me guess, you need ole Sharkster's help."

"Possibly," Millie said. "It depends on whether we can negotiate a deal. We're wondering if you may have noticed any unusual items, boxes or crates being offloaded before we left Miami."

"Yeah. We had a lot of odd stuff taken off the ship. There were bins of broken floor tiles, rolls of commercial carpet, sneeze guards from the buffet, all kinds of junk leftover from the remodel."

"Great," Millie said. "It would have been easy for someone to throw in an extra crate or two without causing suspicion."

Still, even if someone had managed to sneak off the first missing pieces of artwork, there was still one more. "We're here to ask if you could keep your eyes peeled for unusual cartons, boxes or fragile packages someone might try to get off the ship in any of the ports, including San Juan."

Sharky twisted his cigar thoughtfully. "What's in it for the Sharkster?"

"What would you like?" Millie asked.

"Within reason," Annette added.

"Now that you ask, I was just thinkin' this morning how I'm cravin' a homemade beef burrito." Sharky puffed on his cigar and blew a smoke ring into the air. "Smothered in lots and lots of cheese."

He smiled. "And a side of chips with hot sauce. I'm not talking about the namby-pamby sauce. I want the spicy, light-my-lips-on-fire, burnin'-at-both-ends sauce."

Sharky snapped his fingers. "What are those bright red peppers?"

"Ghost peppers?" Annette asked. "You sure you want those? I mean, they'll send you running to the john for days."

"Oh yeah." Sharky rubbed his protruding belly. "Those are the ones."

Annette and Millie exchanged a quick glance. "Okay. So we're agreeing that, in exchange for asking you and your crew to keep an eye out for unusual packages or crates leaving the ship, I'll whip up an extra-large beef burrito smothered in cheese."

"And bring it back at six o'clock tonight," Sharky nodded eagerly.

"Okay." Annette extended her hand and Sharky shook it. "Don't forget the hot sauce and don't bring me a small container. I want enough for leftovers."

"It's a deal."

"Sweet. I'm on the case." Sharky flipped the ignition switch and twisted the handle as he revved up his scooter. "I'll see you gals at six."

Before they could reply, Sharky hit the gas. The tires made a sharp screeching noise right before the scooter backfired.

Millie jumped back and clutched her chest. "I hate it when he does that."

Sharky rounded the corner and disappeared from sight.

"What if Sharky and his men aren't able to help us out?"

"Then we've wasted some perfectly good ghost peppers." Annette shook her head. "I hope he knows what he's asking for."

"I can help you fix Sharky's meal."

"I have to start on the afternoon tea trays first," Annette said. "Tonight is the midnight Mexican buffet so it won't be a big deal, but if you wanna swing by around five, I can always use an extra hand."

"Absolutely." It would give Millie plenty of time to welcome guests back on board the ship and then head to the galley.

They parted ways on deck seven and Millie climbed the stairs to the lido deck to start her rounds.

Many of the ship's passengers had gotten off to spend the day in port so it didn't take long for Millie to check on the staff and crew to make sure everything was running smoothly.

She chatted with Danielle, who was taking a quick break and munching on pizza before heading to guest services or, as Andy liked to call it, "the complaint department."

Andy made a point of checking in with them to monitor guest complaints involving the ship's activities and entertainment.

Nikki, Millie's friend, was working behind the counter so she headed in her direction.

"Hello Millie. How does it feel to fill Andy's shoes?"

Millie rolled her eyes. "Like I've worked an entire week and it's only been a day." She leaned both elbows on the counter. "I'm here to see if any of the passengers have complained about the entertainment."

"Let's see." Nikki narrowed her eyes and tapped the computer screen. "We've logged two complaints. One is that the casino slot machines are too tight."

Millie snorted. "Not much I can do about the slots. What else?"

"That we cancelled the line dancing."

"Next time someone complains about the line dancing, tell them to take it up with Ted Danvers' fiancée, Brigitte."

Nikki wrinkled her nose. "I heard she gave Donovan a list of demands for the staff."

"Yeah. He's been distributing them like candy canes at Christmas. Thankfully, things have been running fairly smoothly today." *Except for being accused of stealing artwork,* Millie silently added. "Even Teddy Danvers seems to be having a good time."

Felippe, one of the ship's security guards, tapped Millie on the shoulder. "I'm sorry to bother you, Miss Millie, but we've got a situation out on the dock and Purser Donovan Sweeney needs you to come out there right away."

Chapter 12

Millie knew as soon as she saw Teddy sitting on the curb with Donovan, Doctor Gundervan, Ted Danvers, Brigitte and Josh huddled around him, something bad had happened during the Segway adventure.

She hurried over to join them. "What's going on?"

"Mr. Appleton decided that Teddy and he should take a little shortcut on their Segways, down a side alley where my son, who has never ridden a Segway, hit a rough section of uneven bricks, was thrown from the contraption and injured his leg." Danvers gazed angrily at Josh. "You should be fired for your stupidity."

"I'm sure it was an accident and not intentional," Donovan said.

"It's no big deal, dad," Teddy said. "And it wasn't Josh's idea. It was mine."

Brigitte flung her arms around Teddy. "You poor thing. You could've hit your head and suffered a skull fracture." She stared at Josh accusingly. "Teddy is a child. You should've known better than to go along with his suggestion."

Captain Armati joined the group. "What happened?"

Donovan filled him in while Captain Armati knelt next to the teen. "I'm sorry to hear of your injury, Teddy and we're all glad you're going to be okay." Captain Armati glanced at Josh. "You're free to board the ship."

"No." Teddy struggled to his feet, waving a plastic bag he was holding. "Josh and I are gonna hang out later. We bought some stuff to build a rocket ship out on the helipad."

He limped to his father's side. "Please Dad? This is the most fun I've ever had on a cruise ship. It was an accident."

Ted Danvers' eyes traveled around the circle before centering on Josh. "I'm going to give you another chance but if one more incident occurs, I'll have you fired and you'll never work on board a Majestic Cruise Lines ship again."

"Yes sir," Josh said solemnly. "I understand."

"I'll bring a pair of crutches to your suite within the hour," Doctor Gundervan promised.

"I don't need crutches." Teddy limped in a slow circle. "See? I'm fine."

"Don't overdo it, Teddy." Ted Danvers followed his son up the entrance ramp while Brigitte and the ship's crew trailed behind.

Josh and Millie were the last in line. "Are you sure you want to do this, Josh?" she whispered.

"Do I have a choice?" Josh whispered back. If Teddy insisted on spending time with Josh and Danvers agreed to it, there was nothing Millie could do.

Josh continued. "Teddy is a good kid. I think he's lonely and crying out for attention. When we're alone, he's like any other teenager but when he's around his dad and Brigitte, it's a completely different story."

Millie wasn't surprised. Her son, Blake, had gone through a similar stage in his teen years when he acted out. Roger, Millie's ex-husband, wasn't a "hands-on" father. He was more concerned with running his business and keeping food on the table than spending time with his children, especially his son.

Years later, Roger tried to make up for lost time but it was too late. The pattern had been set and although father and son got along, they weren't close, not like Millie and her children. The thought of Blake, her daughter, Beth, and her grandchildren caused a sudden lump to form in Millie's throat.

Although Millie had gone home to Michigan not long ago, she was painfully aware she was missing some of those milestones...birthdays, the holidays, Mother's Day. She pushed the sad thoughts aside and patted Josh's arm. "I don't know how I can ever thank you enough for taking on this big responsibility."

Josh grinned. "You owe me one. I'll have to think about how you can pay me back," he teased.

Millie watched as a fresh wave of passengers descended on Danielle, who was welcoming the guests back on board the ship. "I better get back to work."

"Me too." Josh turned to go.

"Call me if you need anything at all Josh."

"I will."

Danielle and Millie spent the next couple of hours greeting the passengers and answering questions.

Millie watched a young couple stagger up the gangway. As they got a closer look, she noticed their splotchy red faces and rushed forward. "Are you okay?"

"I'm feeling dizzy, like I'm going to throw up." The young woman pressed the back of her hand to her forehead.

Millie immediately recognized the symptoms as potential heat stroke. Danielle strode over. "They look overheated."

"Why don't you accompany them to medical as a precaution." The trio disappeared inside one of the elevators and Millie returned to her post.

Thankfully, the rest of the afternoon passed uneventfully and as the embarking crowds thinned, she glanced at her watch.

"It looks like you've got it under control," Millie told Suharto, who was manning the entrance. "I'm going to head upstairs." It was time to help Annette whip up Sharky's smokin' hot salsa and stuffed wet burrito.

***

By the time Millie reached the galley, Annette had already browned the ground beef and added the chopped onion.

"What can I do to help?" Millie snagged an apron from the hook and slipped it over her head. "We have 45 minutes before we meet with Sharky."

"I need some cumin, the dish of chopped garlic over there and some salt and pepper. Oh, and a small can of diced green chili peppers. They're in my office."

Annette's office, aka the dry and canned storage pantry, was unlocked and the light was on. Millie grabbed the requested items, returning to her friend's side moments later.

She watched as Annette dumped and stirred. After she finished mixing the ingredients, she turned the burner off and placed a lid on the pan. "Now we need to mix the Rotel and enchilada sauce. They're over there." Annette pointed to a teetering pyramid of canned goods.

Millie opened the cans and handed them to Annette, who dumped the contents into a saucepan and stirred them over medium heat.

"While I finish heating this, can you warm up one of those tortillas next to the microwave?"

"Sure." Millie placed a large flour tortilla on a glass plate and popped it into the microwave. After it finished warming, she carried the plate to Annette, who spooned a generous amount of browned beef along the center of the tortilla. She sprinkled chopped lettuce and tomato on top of the beef.

"Rolling the tortilla is a little tricky." Annette deftly tucked the side of the flour tortilla under the meat and lettuce mixture before rolling it over and tucking the other end underneath.

Annette grabbed the saucepan and poured sauce along the top so that it pooled on both sides of the burrito. She set the saucepan down, reached for a bag of shredded Mexican blend cheese and added a thick layer to the top. "Last, but not least, chopped green onion."

After sprinkling onion on top of the cheese, Annette placed the plate inside the microwave for 30 seconds until the cheese melted.

Millie grabbed a plate cover and handed it to Annette. "I'll carry the condiments and the hot sauce. Did you make the nuclear hot sauce Sharky requested?"

"Yeah. The sour cream and hot sauce are in to-go cups in the fridge and the tortilla chips are in another to-go box over there."

Millie reached inside the fridge and pulled out the condiment containers before picking up the box of chips. "Ready?"

"As I'll ever be." Annette backed out of the galley and held the door for Millie. "Be careful with the hot sauce. I had to wear gloves, a kitchen mask and goggles to make it."

"You're kidding." Millie glanced at the containers. "It's that hot?"

"Hot enough to burn your britches off." Annette chuckled. "I hope Sharky knows what he's doing."

"Me too." Although Millie liked spicy dishes, they didn't necessarily like her. "I think I'll stick to the mild stuff."

It was slow going to deck zero as Millie cautiously descended the stairs, balancing the condiment containers. They arrived on Sharky's doorstep at six o'clock on the dot.

Annette tapped on the door and reached for the knob.

"C'mon in."

Sharky, along with Reef, the night shift supervisor, were inside the office.

"Did you bring the goods?" Sharky craned his neck and peered over Reef's shoulder.

"Of course." Annette set the room service plate on the edge of the desk.

Millie eased in next to her and set the to-go containers and box of chips next to the covered dish.

Sharky rubbed his hands together and grinned at Reef. "See? You gotta have connections to get the good stuff." He lunged for the room service plate.

"Oh no." Annette tightened her grip on the plate. "We have a deal."

"First, you have to tell us if you were able to track down any special shipments offloaded when we were in port," Millie said.

Sharky rolled his eyes. "Like I told you before, there were a lot of goods going on and off the ship during the dry dock. But, because we had an agreement, I checked with my guys and nobody noticed anything suspicious." He turned to Reef. "You see anything goin' off the ship that looked funny?"

"If I answer the question, do I get some food, too?" Reef asked as he eyed the covered dish.

"Sure you do." Sharky rubbed the sides of his cheeks thoughtfully. "The wet burrito isn't big enough for us to share." He turned to Annette. "Did you remember to bring the chips and hot sauce?"

"Yes."

"Good." Sharky nodded. "I think I'll have more than enough chips and habanero to share."

"I don't..." Millie started to warn Reef about the spicy salsa but quickly changed her mind.

Reef eyed the containers with interest. "No. I didn't see anything during the night shift either. We have to sign for all the goods being brought on board or taken off. If my men had seen something, they would've told me."

"It wasn't the entire week, perhaps maybe sometime late Friday or early Saturday, before we left Miami," Millie said.

"Nope." Reef shook his head.

Millie had a sudden thought. "What about the port stops? Will Siren of the Seas offload anything when we dock in the other ports this week?"

"No." Sharky and Reef said in unison.

"All of the food, the booze, the goods, everything loads in Miami," Reef explained. "Unless we run outta something important. Sometimes those themed cruises will run outta stuff."

Sharky snorted. "Yeah. Remember the time we had a boatload of those Irish folks on board and they ran out of Guinness on day two?" He rolled his eyes. "I though Joe, the beverage supervisor, was gonna lose it. When we stopped in the next port, he spent the entire day buying every single bottle of Guinness on the island."

"I guess we won't worry about port days." Annette and Millie exchanged a quick glance. They didn't have a choice but to believe what Reef and Sharky told them.

"If you come up with something worth sharing, we'd be happy to work another deal," Annette said.

"Like I said, my guys are on the lookout. In the interest of full disclosure, I have to let you know that Patterson was already down here, asking me to keep an eye out for unusual packages. Since he's the top dog, he'll be first on my list to call."

"Why didn't you tell us that before?" Millie asked. "We wouldn't have bothered."

"And miss out on this fabulous feast? Sharky lunged across the desk and snatched the to-go containers and box of tortilla chips from Millie's grasp.

"*I can't wait to try these,*" Sharky sing-songed. He opened the box of chips and pushed it to the center of the desk. "Did you make the sauce like I asked ya?"

"Yes." Annette nodded. "Wearing gloves, a gas mask, goggles and all."

"Sweet." Sharky peeled the lid off the hot sauce container, leaned forward and took a big whiff. He began to gag and his eyes watered. "Perfect." He slid the container toward Reef. "Guests first."

Reef eyed Sharky suspiciously and then reached for a chip. He dipped the chip into the container of red sauce and lifted it to his mouth.

Millie sucked in a breath and waited for the inevitable but Reef appeared completely unfazed as he chewed the chip. "Not bad. Probably could use a little more kick to it."

Reef reached for another chip.

"Gimme that!" Sharky grabbed a chip, dipped it in the hot sauce and shoved the whole thing in his mouth. His eyes bulged and he began to choke.

"Swallow it," Reef advised.

Sharky swallowed the food. "I need water," he gasped as he clutched his throat, his eyes darting around the room. "Water."

Annette raced to the small fridge behind Sharky's desk and flung the door open. She reached inside and pulled out a small container of milk. "I don't see water but you have some milk." She held the bottle up to inspect the contents. 'It looks like it's starting to curdle."

Sharky snatched the plastic milk container, unscrewed the cap and promptly chugged the chunks.

Millie's stomach churned as he downed the thick liquid. "Yuck."

Sharky slammed the empty container on the counter and squeezed his eyes shut as sweat poured down his face.

He doubled over and clutched his stomach. "Oh..."

"Are you all right?" Millie leaned across the desk, careful to avoid making contact with the spicy hot sauce.

Instead of answering, Sharky dropped his head in his hands and began to moan.

The trio watched silently until finally Sharky lifted his head and wiped his face with his shirtsleeve. "Whew. This stuff is potent. I think I'll have another." He reached for a chip and Millie stared in disbelief as he dipped it in the hot sauce.

Reef, unfazed by Sharky's reaction, dipped another chip in the sauce and chewed the end. "I need to get the recipe for this stuff."

Annette shook her head. "I need to head upstairs to help with first seating."

"I should get back to work too," Millie said. The women reminded Sharky and Reef of their promise to keep an eye out for special crates or packages and then exited Sharky's office.

Millie waited until they were in the stairwell before she spoke. "We can't depend on those two to help us track down the thief or thieves. I have another idea."

Chapter 13

"We'll have to discuss your idea later," Annette said. "I'm sure Amit is ready to pull his hair out, what little he has."

"I need to get back to work, too." Millie thanked Annette for helping her out and then radioed Danielle to check on the status of the passengers she suspected were on the verge of a heat stroke. She was relieved to find out they were going to recover.

Millie had just enough time to grab a bite to eat from the ship's deli before the first headliner show started. The show, one of Millie's favorites, featured a medley of songs and dance from the 70's era.

Much to her relief, both shows went off without a hitch. After the shows ended, Millie made her rounds, stopping briefly to chat with Cat and then finally, after the clubs opened and her shift ended, headed to her cabin.

The next morning, their first full day at sea, passed by in a blur as Millie moved from Pierre LeBlanc's wine tasting presentation, always a hit with the passengers, to bingo in the theater.

Lunch consisted of a burger on the go and then Millie headed to the Tahitian Nights Dance Club where the ballroom dancing class was being held.

Millie took a step inside, hoping to catch a glimpse of Brigitte, but the woman wasn't there. She glanced at her watch and then made her way over to the bar where she climbed onto one of the barstools.

Bobby, one of the bartenders, sidled over. "Hello Miss Millie. Are you going to join the class?"

"Not this time. I'm here to make sure everything is running smoothly." She eyed a row of soda cans on the back of the bar. "Do you think you could spare a Diet Coke?"

"Of course." Bobby filled a glass with ice. "I hope more guests show up. There aren't very many." He opened a can of soda, poured some into the glass and placed both in front of her.

"No there aren't." Millie sipped her soda and surveyed the crowd. She stayed long enough to finish her Diet Coke and concluded that Brigitte, the person who had insisted Siren of the Seas offer a ballroom dancing class, was not even going to show up.

"Thanks for the soda." Millie slid off the stool and nearly collided with someone who was standing directly behind her. "What are you doing here?"

"I hoped you would be happy to see me," Captain Armati teased.

"I...Of course I am. I'm just surprised."

"A little birdie told me I might find you down here." Nic motioned to the dance floor. "Would you care to dance?"

Millie's pulse quickened. She had never danced with Captain Armati before, except for a couple of spins around his living room floor after one of their dinner dates. "I..."

"I'll take that as a yes." He slipped an arm around Millie's waist and guided her to the floor. Several of the other passengers stopped to gaze at the couple. It wasn't every day the captain of the ship joined passengers in an activity.

Captain Armati smiled and nodded at those closest to them before he swept his bride-to-be into his arms and began twirling her around the floor. As if by magic, the lights in the club lowered and small sparkles from the overhead disco ball began to dance around the room.

Millie had taken ballroom dancing lessons years ago but she was rusty to say the least, although no one would have guessed as they watched the striking couple circle the floor. It was as if they had danced together for years.

Nic lowered his head close to hers. "I love you."

Millie's heart skipped a beat and she tightened her grip on his arm. "I love you too." She closed her eyes and savored the sweet moment.

Too soon, the music ended and they took a step back, only to realize the other dancers had circled them and began to applaud.

Emeline, the instructor, hurried over. "You two should teach a ballroom dancing class, not me. It was magical watching you."

Millie's cheeks warmed and she gave her handsome captain a shy smile. "Maybe we should."

The captain escorted Millie off the dance floor and they made their way into the lobby. "There will be more moments like this," he said. "Many more if I have my way."

"I hope so," Millie said breathlessly. "Were you really looking for me?"

"I was on my way to meet with the safety supervisor when I heard someone on the radio mention you were in the Tahitian Nights Dance Club supervising the ballroom dancing and I couldn't resist."

"It was a wonderful surprise." If they had been alone, Millie would have stepped into Nic's arms. "I miss you," she whispered.

"I miss you too." Nic squeezed her hand. "I heard there's some artwork missing from High Seas Gallery and Brenda Parcore, the manager, is blaming Andy and now you."

"Yes. Andy isn't here to defend himself. Apparently, I was the last person to lay eyes on an expensive painting that suddenly vanished." Millie grimaced. "I think Ms. Parcore is setting us up."

"I'm sure Patterson will get to the bottom of it."

"Someone will," Millie muttered under her breath.

Nic wagged his finger at her. "Don't you have enough on your plate this week?"

Millie's eyes widened innocently. "All I'm doing is a little preliminary poking around. It's nothing to be concerned about."

The couple strolled to the center of the ship where Nic reluctantly paused. "Promise me you'll stay out of trouble."

"I'll try," Millie said before watching Nic descend the stairs and disappear from sight.

After the dinner hour, Danielle offered to swap the evening rounds in exchange for co-hosting Killer Karaoke and Millie gratefully accepted.

In between karaoke sets, Millie mulled over the missing artwork. She suspected someone who worked in the gallery was somehow involved in the thefts. Motive and opportunity. Motive would be money and opportunity would be the fact the employees knew there were no surveillance cameras inside the gallery.

As subcontractors, the High Seas employees were not required to report to Majestic Cruise Lines. The cruise line had no control over High Seas

Gallery's policies and procedures, other than to make sure the gallery employees obeyed all of the ship's rules.

Sneaking the artwork off during the dry dock project was near genius. As Sharky and Reef pointed out, so many different crates, boxes and materials had changed hands and made their way on and off the ship, it would be nearly impossible for someone to spot something being offloaded that looked out of place.

The fact that another piece had gone missing after the ship departed from Miami was Millie's only hope the thief or thieves would be caught. The ship's next stop was St. Thomas the following day and perhaps the thieves would try to get the goods off the ship while in port.

Despite Sharky and Reef's promise to be on the lookout, Millie wasn't sure how reliable they were.

The evening's special entertainment was the comedy show, which was usually standing room only. Andy had tossed around the idea of distributing tickets since they'd received numerous complaints from passengers that the venue was too small.

After making sure that all of the activities were running smoothly, Millie wandered into the galley. It was a beehive of activity so she stood off to the side and watched as the kitchen crew began assembling large trays of chips and salsa for the midnight Mexican buffet.

She smiled as she remembered Sharky and Reef's reaction to the spicy salsa and wondered if there were any lingering effects from eating the super spicy dish.

Finally, the rush to get the dishes up on the lido deck tapered off and Annette wandered over. "You'd think after all this time I'd be used to the frantic pace, but there are times, like now, I want nothing more than to kick my shoes off, put my feet up, turn the television on and veg out."

"Me too," Millie said. "Especially this week."

"No news from Patterson on the missing art?"

"Nope." Millie shook her head. "I've been thinking. It must have been a piece of cake to get the first few pieces of stolen art off the ship. With all of the materials moved on and off the ship during the dry dock renovations, no one would notice an extra package or two."

"True," Annette agreed.

"Maybe the thieves got brave or brazen. They got away with it once. Why not try again?" Millie tapped the countertop. "I'm almost certain it's an inside job by one of the employees who works in the art gallery."

"Brenda Parcore," Annette said.

"Yeah, but Brenda is such an obvious suspect. Don't you think she'd be a little more stealth?" Millie asked. "She admitted she's the only one with keys and the only one who knows the combination to the safe."

Annette removed her apron and folded it in half. "Do you know anything about the others who work in the gallery?"

Millie briefly told her what she knew, how Merlin Cuspet had worked for High Seas Gallery for two years and before that, for a competitor.

She knew little about Yasmin Odo, other than she'd worked for the company less than a year.

"Stanley Zelchon is the most intriguing of the three. He joined the ship this week. I found an article online about him. He used to be a fine arts auctioneer for a large, global art dealer."

"Why would he want to work in a small gallery on board a cruise ship?"

"My thoughts exactly." Millie shrugged. "I met him briefly. He's very knowledgeable about packing art for transportation and I noted a hint of disdain in his voice when he mentioned Brenda Parcore's name."

She continued. "If only there was some way we could find out a little more about the High Seas Gallery employees."

"I have an idea," Annette said. "What if we knew a rich passenger, a customer who was shopping for a high end piece of art to add to their collection?"

"That would be great, but Parcore has seen Danielle and me. I'm sure she would recognize Cat and probably even you. None of us own clothes that could pass for high end." Millie sighed. "It's impossible. I guess I could try searching the internet again."

Annette crossed her arms and gazed at Millie thoughtfully. "Tomorrow is a port day. We'll be in St. Thomas..."

"From eight in the morning until five."

"Perfect." Annette snapped her fingers. "Come by here around 1:30 tomorrow."

"It should be a fairly quiet day. I wonder if Danvers, his son and Brigitte plan to get off in port." Millie unclipped her radio from her belt. "Josh, do you copy?"

"Go ahead Millie."

"Can you please call me at..." Millie pointed at the phone on the galley wall.

"7122," Annette whispered.

"Extension 7122."

"10-4."

The phone rang moments later and Millie answered. "I thought I would check in to see how it was going with Teddy."

"I see. Good. I'm glad to hear it. Are you getting off in St. Thomas tomorrow?" Millie paused. "So Mr. Danvers and Brigitte are getting off for a golf excursion but you and Teddy are staying on board. Thank you for the update. Can you meet me for breakfast at 7:00 in the crew dining room?"

Josh promised he would be there. Millie thanked him again and told him good-bye.

Annette gave a thumbs-up. "Perfect. You should have a quiet day tomorrow. I have someone who can pull off going incognito and glean some information from the gallery employees tomorrow."

"What if the gallery is closed and no one is working?" Millie plucked the Cruise Ship Chronicles schedule from her back pocket and rifled through the sheets of paper. "Ah. They'll be open from 2 p.m. until 10 p.m."

"Even better." Annette beamed. "Meet me up here at 1:30 tomorrow afternoon."

"What do you have up your sleeve?" Millie asked.

"You'll see," Annette said mysteriously. "All you have to do is show up at 1:30 tomorrow. I'll take care of the rest."

Chapter 14

Millie drifted restlessly around the lido deck, watching as the passengers enjoyed the evening's festivities. She hoped Annette's secret plan would work and they would be able to glean more information out of the High Seas Gallery employees. It was worth a shot.

Although all the clues pointed to Brenda Parcore, something was off. She was too obvious of a suspect. The fact that Stanley Zelchon had just joined the ship and previously worked as an auctioneer for a prestigious art auction house was suspect.

It was too much of a coincidence that the first pieces of art went missing at almost the same time that Zelchon boarded the ship to begin working.

Wouldn't he be better suited for an office position? Working on a cruise ship wasn't necessarily a dead end job or a step down, but it certainly wasn't a career advancement.

There was also Merlin Cuspet. He previously worked for a competitor. Perhaps he had decided it was worth the risk to steal valuable artwork, especially if he could pin it on his boss, Brenda.

It led to another question...perhaps Brenda's co-workers didn't like her and were trying to set her up. She hadn't given Millie a warm and fuzzy feeling.

Last, but not least, was Yasmin Odo. Millie knew very little about the woman.

Millie's cabin was empty, and although it was late, Danielle wasn't home yet so she decided to indulge in a long, hot shower.

After showering, Millie plopped in front of the desk mirror and began towel drying her hair. She thought of her impromptu dance with Nic. *Would* they be able to marry and stay on board the ship together?

Millie hoped to get into Ted Danvers' good graces, to butter him up so that Nic and she could present him with their special request.

Her heart skipped a beat as she thought about the missing artwork. What if Brenda Parcore tracked down Danvers and told him she suspected the cruise director and assistant cruise director were involved in the art heist?

What if the company started an internal investigation and placed Millie on leave? A jolt of pure terror pierced Millie's heart. She couldn't let that happen.

She needed to bounce her thoughts off someone who was experienced in investigating crimes, someone with more experience than she had.

Roger, Millie's ex-husband, may have been able to help but he still blamed her for his fiancée, Delilah Osborne's, death. It suddenly dawned on Millie there was someone else and that someone was her cousin, Gloria Rutherford-Kennedy.

As soon as the ship docked in St. Thomas and Millie had cell service, she was going to give her cousin a call.

***

Millie watched as a bleary-eyed Josh set his tray on the table and slid into the seat across from her. "You look like I feel."

"I checked my email last night before I went to bed. My brother, Alan, made it to Miami. He said Mom has another doctor's appointment today so I'm stressed out about that."

"I'm so sorry Josh," Millie said. "I've been praying for your mom and for your family."

"Thanks, Millie." Josh unwrapped his silverware and placed the napkin in his lap. "At least keeping an eye on Teddy has taken my mind off some of my own problems." He nodded at Millie. "I heard the woman who runs the art gallery is making her rounds, questioning the staff about some missing artwork."

"Yeah. It's a mess. For some reason, she seems to think Andy and I are involved since we were around two of the pieces of art just before they went missing."

"Maybe you should stay away from the art gallery," Josh joked.

"No kidding." Millie shifted the subject to the Danvers family, curious to get Josh's take on the family dynamics. "How is it going with Teddy and the Danvers family?"

"From outward appearances, Teddy seems to be a troublemaker, but I don't think that's the case. He's crying out for attention from his father." Josh glanced around and lowered his voice. "I'm not 100% certain, but I think Teddy intentionally fell off the Segway."

"He did?" Millie blinked rapidly as she digested the information. She'd heard of people who purposely injured themselves. "There's a name for people who self-harm."

"It's called Munchausen. I'm beginning to suspect this might be the case. I don't think Teddy and Brigitte get along."

"I'm not surprised." Brigitte appeared to be much younger than Ted. In fact, now that Millie thought about it, the woman was probably closer to Teddy's age than his father's age. "I wonder how long the two of them have been engaged."

Josh lifted a brow.

"They're not engaged?"

"You didn't hear me say that."

Millie shook her head. "Whether she is or isn't, I think you better be extra cautious when you're with Teddy."

"I agree, which is why I told him I wasn't going to get off the ship today. I can't chance it."

Once again, Millie was consumed by guilt over strong-arming Josh into taking Teddy under his wing. "Are you sure you don't want me to find someone to replace you?"

"No." Josh sawed off the end of his omelet. "I promised Teddy we would build a rocket later today and give it a test run out near the helipad."

"Will security allow you to shoot off a rocket?"

"Yeah. I already ran it by them. It's harmless. The rocket is a 2-litre plastic Coke bottle." Josh went on to explain he planned to use a mixture of vinegar and baking soda to propel the rocket and how he'd made one when he was Teddy's age.

"I might have to check it out. What time are you planning to launch the rocket?"

"Later this morning. You want me to give you a buzz on your radio?"

"Sure." Millie popped the last of her crispy hash brown bite into her mouth. "I need to head down to the gangway to see passengers off." She shoved her chair back. "Thanks for meeting me, Josh, and thanks for helping me out this week."

"You're welcome, Millie. I think you're doing a great job of filling in for Andy. The rest of the entertainment crew does, too."

The last couple of days had been so chaotic, Millie wasn't sure if she was coming or going and hadn't given much thought to how well she was doing – she was just trying to survive. "Thanks, Josh. I have a greater appreciation for everything Andy does and it makes me love my own job even more."

On her way out, Millie placed her empty breakfast plate in the bin and her utensils in the tray next to it.

The fact that Brigitte and Ted weren't necessarily heading to the altar made sense. Millie wondered how many other women had been in young Teddy's life.

The cruise was almost half over and she was beginning to think she would survive as long as there were no other crises with the Danvers and she could figure out who was stealing the artwork from the gallery.

The rest of the morning passed quickly. Many of the guests got off in St. Thomas and Millie couldn't blame them. It was a beautiful island and a popular Caribbean cruise port. One of the island's main draws was the gorgeous Magen's Bay, often described as one of the most beautiful beaches in the world, and known for its white sandy beaches and crystal clear water.

Coki Beach, next door to the Coral World Ocean Park, was another popular beach. Although Millie had never visited Coki Beach, she'd heard it was a great spot for snorkeling and diving.

The beach area also had a beach side restaurant. Coki Beach was on Millie's to-do list, but it looked as if it would be on the list for a while longer since the Siren of the Seas was picking up a different itinerary.

Josh paged Millie close to eleven to tell her Teddy and he were at the "launch pad," the ship's helipad, located near the bow of the ship and on deck five forward. She found the two of them huddled in the center of the bright yellow ring.

Teddy glanced up when he heard Millie approach. She grinned when she spotted the plastic goggles he was wearing. At least Josh was taking the "safety first" motto seriously.

"This is gonna be awesome."

Millie took a step forward for a closer look. Although the body of the rocket was clear, the fins were bright green and made of a thick foam material.

"Are you ready?" Josh asked Teddy.

"Yeah."

"Okay. Stand back." Josh waited until Teddy and Millie were a safe distance before he snapped the lid onto the canister, flipped it over and then jogged over to join them.

The half-full container began to fizz before making a loud popping noise and rocketing into the air.

Liquid sprayed down and spattered the trio. A strong vinegar odor filled the air.

"Whoops. I forgot how much liquid sprays out." Josh swiped at the liquid on his forehead. "I'm sorry Millie."

"It's okay." Millie used the sleeve of her shirt to wipe her face.

"Can we do it again?" Teddy asked.

"Maybe later," Josh said. "First we'll have to clean up and then check to make sure we have enough supplies left."

Millie congratulated the two on their successful launch mission and headed to a quiet section of the outdoor deck area.

The area was open to passengers except when security closed it off for emergency medical evacuations, which thankfully wasn't often. The majority of guests had no idea it was there and even if they did, how to get to it.

Millie had programmed her cousin's cell phone number in her phone the last time she'd seen her, which was when Gloria and her group of friends had cruised on board the Siren of the Seas.

She pulled her cell phone from her pocket and scrolled through her contacts list until she found her cousin's name. Millie pressed the call button and prayed Gloria would answer. It went to voice mail.

"Hi Gloria. It's me – Millie. I'm sure you're surprised to hear from me. Our ship is docked in St. Thomas today so I have cell service." She glanced at her watch. "It's 12:30 now and I'll have my phone on for about an hour. If you get this message and could please give me a call back by 1:30, I would appreciate it." She rattled off her cell phone number and thanked Gloria before disconnecting the line.

186

While she waited, Millie called her son, Blake, and left him a message.

Her next call was to her daughter, Beth, who answered on the first ring. "Hi Mom. How's it going?"

"Good. Andy is on leave this week so I'm busy running the entertainment end of things."

"That's right. You mentioned Andy was leaving last week."

Mother and daughter chatted about Millie's grandkids, Beth's husband, David, and the weather in Michigan. Beth had stopped asking her mother about the weather because it was always the same...sunny and hot.

Half the time, Millie didn't even know what month it was, except for the holidays, when they decorated the ship for Christmas, and spring break, when Siren of the Seas was packed with college kids and school-age children.

Spring break was right around the corner; another reason the ship had completed the renovations before the busy summer season kicked in.

"How's the weather?" Millie asked.

"Yesterday it was in the 60's and they're forecasting flurries tomorrow," Beth reported. "I would ask you how the weather is, but I already know. It's sunny and gorgeous."

"Yes, it is, but don't forget, we'll be getting into hurricane season soon." Millie already had one hurricane season under her belt. The ship had run into a tropical depression in Nassau and hadn't been able to dock.

Captain Armati had shifted course and managed to escape the brunt of the storm but it had been a rough ride for several hours.

They chatted for a little while longer, until Millie's phone beeped. It was Gloria. "Oh Beth. I hate to cut you off but Gloria is on the other line."

"Cousin Gloria?"

"Yeah. Gotta go. I'll call you on Saturday when we're back in Miami." Millie told her daughter she loved her before disconnecting the call.

"Gloria?"

"Hi Millie. How are you?"

"Fine. Okay. Well. Not really, but first, how are you?"

The women quickly ran through the pleasantries until Gloria couldn't stand it any longer. "So I'm dying to find out why you called. Let me guess, you and your handsome captain couldn't wait to get married so you eloped."

"I wish," Millie sighed. "We're still working on it. There's something else. I have a bit of a problem." She briefly explained the situation with Brenda Parcore and the missing artwork, how the woman seemed the perfect suspect but something wasn't adding up.

It was quiet on the other end of the line. "Gloria?"

"Yes. I'm still here. I'm thinking."

Woof.

"Mally, I'll be done in a minute. Sorry Millie. Spring is almost here and the squirrels are driving Mally crazy."

"I bet." Millie grinned.

"Back to your dilemma. You say that this Brenda..."

"Parcore," Millie prompted.

"Parcore is the only one with keys to the display cases and she's the only one who knows the combination to the safe. Could it be she lost her key at one time and someone made a copy of it?"

Millie hadn't thought of that angle. It was possible. It was also possible that Brenda wouldn't admit to losing the key. "I don't know. I suppose. I'm meeting Annette shortly. We're working on an undercover operation to try to glean more clues from the other art gallery employees."

"You know my motto," Gloria said. "Motive and opportunity. Motive, of course, is money and opportunity would be one of the gallery employees, someone who knows the value of the stolen artwork."

"There's one thing I forgot to mention. Each of the pieces was stolen from clear display frames."

"What about surveillance cameras?" Gloria asked.

"Nope. They didn't catch anything."

The women discussed the possibilities at length, until it was time for Millie to start her rounds.

"I wish I was there to help you, Millie. The artwork didn't walk off by itself. The fact that at least one of the pieces was stolen after the ship sailed is a clue." Gloria paused. "If I were you, I would focus on this Zelchon person. His story isn't adding up. Prestigious art auctioneers do not suddenly quit their jobs just to join a cruise ship."

Millie thanked her cousin for calling her back and after she hung up the phone, Gloria's final words rang in her ear and confirmed Millie's suspicions. They needed to take a closer look at Stanley Zelchon.

Chapter 15

Millie resolved a minor crisis with an irate passenger who insisted the rock-climbing wall open up while the ship was in port before handling a discrepancy with a batch of bingo cards.

Her next stop was to check in on "Cruise Clue," the adult mystery and scavenger hunt Kevin was hosting.

She wrapped up her rounds at approximately 1:30, the time she'd promised to meet Annette in the galley.

Grace, one of the galley workers, was in the salad prep area, chopping tomatoes and gave Millie a quick wave.

Annette was nowhere in sight so Millie headed to the open walk-in freezer and stuck her head inside. It was empty.

She stepped back out and zigzagged around the counters until she reached Amit. "Have you seen Annette?"

"Sort of," Amit said.

"We were supposed to meet at 1:30."

"Who are you looking for darling?"

Millie spun around and almost collided with a woman wearing a beautifully tailored black tuxedo pantsuit with satin sleeve cuffs and pocket flaps.

The blonde woman's ankles wobbled as she took a tentative step forward, teetering precariously on high heels.

"I-uh." Millie squinted her eyes and leaned forward. The woman's face was familiar. "Annette?"

The blonde grinned. "Almost didn't recognize me did you?"

"Oh my gosh." Millie tapped one of the satin sleeve cuffs. "What a gorgeous outfit. Where did you get this?"

"I...borrowed it." Annette quickly changed the subject. "These heels are killing me. You're gonna have to help me navigate."

Annette slowly tottered out of the galley and Millie trailed behind. They moved at a snail's pace as they walked down the long corridor and by the time they reached the bank of elevators and stairs, Annette had developed a slight limp.

"You're limping." Millie pointed out the obvious.

"The shoes are a tad small, but they'll have to do. Thank the Lord I didn't have to wear a dress." For some mysterious reason, Annette had an aversion to dresses. "You're gonna have to take the elevator this time. There's no way I can navigate the stairs."

Millie nodded. "It's only one deck down." The women stepped inside an empty elevator. "You'll have to tell me later where you got the outfit."

Several guests joined them. They rode in silence and waited until the passengers vacated the elevator to follow them out into the lobby. When they reached the other side of the art gallery, Millie halted. "I'll wait out here."

"Okay." Annette teetered toward the gallery.

"Hey."

"Yeah?"

"Break a leg," Millie joked.

Annette rolled her eyes.

"Seriously, though, I think Zelchon knows something," Millie whispered.

Annette gave her a thumbs-up and plodded to the art gallery entrance. She straightened her wig, took a deep breath and stepped inside.

***

Annette swept, or more like stumbled, inside the art gallery and eased the door shut behind her. Despite the crisp, cool air inside the gallery showroom, little droplets of sweat began to form on her brow.

She tugged on her wig to make sure it was still in place before attempting to glide across the carpeted floor.

"May I help you?"

Annette turned a little too quickly and began flailing wildly before clamping onto the corner of a display panel. "I thought I would drop by to check out your paintings. I'm looking for a specific piece of art."

"Oh?" The petite brown-haired woman placed both hands behind her back. "Do you know the artist's name?"

"Uhm...It's on the tip of my tongue."

"Perhaps if you could describe the painting to me."

"Yes." Annette nodded. "It's a vase...with flowers. Tall flowers." She knew she sounded like an idiot but had no idea she was going to have to answer specific questions. After years of being employed by the National Security Agency, it was apparent she'd finally lost her edge. "I would know it if I saw it." She glanced at the young woman's nametag, Yasmin Odo.

"I'm sorry – Yasmin." Annette began fanning her face. "I think the heat is getting to me."

"Oh?" A concerned look crossed Yasmin's face. "We keep the temperature at sixty-eight degrees in here. Perhaps you're getting ill." She took a step back.

"No, I mean, I don't think I'm getting sick. My throat is a little parched." Annette pressed her hand to her throat.

"Let me get you some water." The young woman hurried across the gallery and out of sight.

Annette limped to the nearby wall of art and spotted a portrait of a large vase with flowers. She bent down to examine the signature. "Jean Paul DeWeith," she whispered. Annette mentally repeated the name as she hurried to resume her spot.

Yasmin returned, accompanied by a tall, dark-haired man.

"Ms. Odo told me you were feeling ill." The man handed Annette a glass of water.

"Thank you." Annette gulped the water. "I'm feeling much better."

"She said you were looking for a specific work of art, flowers in a vase," the man said. "Perhaps if you could be a little more descriptive."

"Of course." Annette smiled. "I think the water has cleared my head. It was by an artist whose name is Jean Paul De...something."

"Jean Paul DeWeith."

Yasmin interrupted. "We have one of his still life paintings over here." She pointed to the painting Annette had just examined.

"Ah. It looks like the piece." Annette nodded. "I don't know much about Mr. DeWeith's works and was hoping someone here could shed a little light on this particular artist."

"My knowledge of original works isn't nearly as vast as Mr. Zelchon's knowledge," Yasmin said.

A customer wandered in and Yasmin glanced at Zelchon. "If you like you can assist Ms.?"

"Tammy Clapboard." Annette extended a hand. "I am so sorry. Where are my manners?"

Yasmin shook Annette's hand before excusing herself.

Zelchon turned his attention to Annette. "Are you adding to your collection, Ms. Clapboard?"

"Perhaps. I've recently begun studying art." *Today,* she silently added.

"I see. Art appreciation is a passion of mine."

"Oh? Have you been in the art business long?" *It was like taking candy from a baby.*

"Yes. I've been in the business for many years." He changed the subject. "DeWeith was a 16th century artist." Zelchon shared with her the artist's brief history before droning on about the piece.

"It's lovely. At the risk of sounding crass, how much is it?"

"Four thousand, three hundred dollars," Zelchon replied. He studied her face for her reaction.

"It seems reasonable," Annette said.

"We provide each buyer with a certificate of authenticity."

"Perfect." She studied the piece. "I can't imagine painting a picture that people would actually pay for. Out of curiosity, what is the most expensive piece you've ever sold?"

"Fourteen million. It sold in less than twenty minutes." He paused. "Ah, the art of the auction."

"It sounds as if you enjoy auctioning art," Annette said.

"I do."

"So I take it you auction the art here on the ship?"

"Yes. I prefer land-based auctions," he said. "I'm only on the ship temporarily." He steered the subject back to art and Annette knew if she asked too many questions, he was going to become suspicious.

There was one other person Annette hadn't met yet...Merlin Cuspet. "I'd like to look around for a few moments, if you don't mind."

"At your leisure." Zelchon smiled. "I'll be in the back if something else strikes your fancy."

Annette thanked him and began slowly circling the gallery. She caught a glimpse of another man who was standing in the back of the gallery, his attention focused on a computer in front of him.

With Zelchon out of the picture, Annette knew this was her chance. She stumbled across the room, mentally cursing the shoes with every painful step she took.

The man looked up as Annette approached the desk. "Can I help you?"

"Yes. I was wondering if I might ask you a question." She glanced at the man's nametag, *Merlin Cuspet*.

"Certainly," Cuspet replied. "What's your question?"

"If I purchased a piece of art, what is the process for getting it home?"

"All of our pieces are carefully packaged. Let me show you."

Cuspet led Annette to the corner of the gallery. He opened a closet door and switched the light on. "Each painting is individually wrapped. We use special padding and crating to avoid moisture and heat." He demonstrated the packing method.

"You seem to know a lot about art. Have you worked for High Seas Gallery long?"

The man placed the packing materials on top of a stack of crates. "Yes, for a couple of years. I worked for another gallery prior to taking this position. I specialized in high-end pieces at an art gallery on the West Coast. California to be exact." He continued. "I'm more familiar with contemporary pieces such as Miles Davison."

"Do you miss working in California?"

"Sometimes." He shrugged. "But I won't be going back there anytime soon."

"You must love working on the cruise ship then," Annette said.

"Not necessarily. If Brenda Parcore, the manager, leaves High Seas Gallery, I'll be taking her place."

Chapter 16

"Brenda Parcore?" Annette asked.

"She runs this art gallery. She mentioned perhaps moving to corporate after her contract ends." Cuspet lowered his voice. "I wasn't supposed to repeat that,"

"I don't know Ms. Parcore," Annette said. *Very well,* she silently added.

Cuspet glanced around nervously. "I better get back to work."

Annette knew the conversation was over and Cuspet regretted his minor slip. She thanked him for his time and told him she wanted to mull over her decision before slinking out of the gallery.

She slid the door open and nearly collided with a woman who was making her way inside.

"Excuse me," the petite blonde said as she stepped aside. "They need to remove these silly sheer curtains so customers can see where they're going."

"I agree." Annette nodded and started to ease past the woman.

"Hey." The woman pointed at Annette's jacket. "I have an identical Armani suit. It's the exact same color and everything."

Annette laughed nervously and tugged on the edge of the jacket. "And I thought I was buying a one-of-a-kind, not an off-the-rack ensemble."

"Me too," the woman said. "What a rip-off."

"If you'll excuse me." Annette turned on her heel and hurried down the hall. She could feel the heat from the woman's stare...a woman she was certain was Danvers' fiancée, Brigitte.

Millie popped out of an alcove and fell into step. "How did it go?"

"Great, except I need to get this outfit down to the laundry area ASAP."

"I thought you were kidding when you said you borrowed it. So the outfit isn't yours?"

"Of course not," Annette snapped. "It would cost me a month's salary to buy this getup and where would I wear it?"

"W-who does it belong to?" Millie asked the question but she had a sinking feeling she already knew the answer.

"Danvers' fiancée. I bumped into her outside the gallery. I think she's suspicious, which is why I need to get this back to the laundry area stat."

The women hustled at a fast clip and finally reached the stairs.

"Wait a sec." Annette stopped abruptly, removed the high-heeled shoes and then flew down the stairs at breakneck speed.

"Brigitte sent this in for dry cleaning. You went down there to find an outfit to wear for your disguise and it just so happens that you picked Brigitte's outfit."

"I didn't *know* it was Brigitte's outfit when I took it and I certainly didn't think I would run into her while I was wearing it. You said she was getting off the ship."

"I thought she was," Millie said breathlessly.

They jogged down the long hall until they reached the laundry area.

Annette flung the doors open and began unbuttoning the jacket. She shrugged it off and began unzipping the slacks.

"You're going to strip down right here?"

"Yeah. These guys aren't looking." Annette nodded at a couple of the crewmembers who were spreading pool towels along the top of an enormous conveyor belt.

Millie snatched a flat sheet from a pile of dirty laundry and held it up to form a makeshift curtain.

After Annette stripped down, she tossed the outfit to Millie and hurried over to a corner cubby. She pulled a chef's uniform from the shelf and began dressing. "It's like it never happened."

Annette fastened the last shirt button and reached for her work shoes.

"You're back." One of the laundry crewmembers wandered over.

"I am, Rahul. Thanks for the loan of the outfit," Annette said. "I'll send Amit down with your butter chicken and kaali daal within the hour."

The man took the discarded outfit from Millie and bowed. "Thank you Miss Annette. Thank you vedi much."

Millie waited until they were in the hall to talk. "What is kaali daal?"

"Black lentils. It's a popular Indian dish." They climbed the metal stairs to deck two. "If I keep this up, I'm gonna have a whole section of the galley set aside to fix food dishes to bribe the crew."

"Thanks Annette. I had no idea you borrowed the outfit from the laundry department." Millie grinned. "I wonder what would have happened if Brigitte knew you were wearing her outfit."

"She's suspicious, which is close enough," Annette said. "I'll bet money she's going to have her room steward tracking it down shortly." She wiped her brow. "That was a close one."

"So what did you find out?" Millie grasped the handrail.

"I almost immediately crossed Yasmin Odo off the list. She doesn't know much about art and hasn't worked on the ship long. She tried to help me and then turned me over to Stanley Zelchon."

Annette went on to explain that, at first, Zelchon seemed the most likely suspect. It didn't make sense for the man, who once held a prestigious auctioneer position, to quit and take a job on board a cruise ship. "The commissions alone."

She rolled her eyes. "He would be crazy to leave a high paying job to join a cruise ship. It still doesn't add up."

"So you think it may be Zelchon?" Millie asked.

"It's possible. There's also Merlin Cuspet, who once worked for a competitor. He let it slip he is in line to take Brenda Parcore's job."

Millie's eyes widened. "Parcore is quitting?"

"Cuspet said she was considering a transfer to the corporate office and he was in line to take her place."

"So maybe it's Cuspet. He's trying to set Brenda up so she'll leave," Millie said.

"Or it's Brenda, knowing she's on her way out. Or Zelchon, or maybe even Yasmin. Always suspect the least suspect."

The women climbed the stairs. "We're back to square one," Millie groaned. "Thanks for helping out, Annette. I don't know what I would do without you."

"You'd be wearing stiletto heels and making a fool of yourself."

They parted ways on deck seven and Millie wandered to the buffet area to fix a plate of food. She circled the eating area in search of a quiet table when she spotted Josh alone and eating chilidogs.

"Mind if I join you?" Millie asked.

"Of course not." Josh pulled out the chair next to him and patted the seat. "I was going to radio you as soon as I finished eating to see if you had anything for me to do the rest of the afternoon."

"I thought you were hanging out with Teddy." Millie transferred her plate of food to the table and propped the empty tray against her chair.

"We hung out this morning. Teddy was supposed to check in with his dad before noon, before his father and Brigitte left the ship. We were a little late and Brigitte went crazy."

"Did she fire you?"

"No." Josh shook his head. "They grounded Teddy. He has to stay in the cabin the rest of the afternoon."

"Wow. I had no idea they were that strict." Millie picked up a chicken tender and dipped it in her ranch dressing.

"Neither did I." The conversation drifted to the homemade rocket and Millie complimented Josh's creativity.

"Thanks. Science has always been my first love. Entertaining people is my second." They chatted about life on board the ship. Josh asked Millie about her family and if they were coming down for the wedding.

"If there is a wedding." Millie absentmindedly swirled the ice in her glass. "Captain Armati and I planned to present Mr. Danvers with the petition during dinner at the captain's table on the last night of the cruise but now that I know him a little better, I'm beginning to think it won't make an iota of difference."

"I dunno, Millie. I think Ted Danvers is a reasonable man, but his girlfriend, Brigitte?" Josh blew air through thinned lips. "She's another story."

"So you're certain they're not engaged?"

"I'm certain. Teddy said as much this morning. He said he hopes his dad doesn't marry her."

Millie mulled over Josh's statements. Perhaps Brigitte was pushing for a proposal and viewed Teddy as an obstacle in her way. Meanwhile, poor Teddy was crying out for his father's attention. It was a sad situation. "I'm sorry you got caught up in their family problems, as if you don't already have enough of your own."

She changed the subject. "If you want something to do, I could use another person up here to lend a hand with the afternoon pool party games."

"Sounds good." Josh tossed his napkin on top of his empty plate. "I'll check back with Teddy again later," he promised before walking away.

The rest of the early afternoon passed quickly and before Millie knew it, it was time to head to the gangway to greet guests who were returning to the ship.

Danielle joined her moments later. "I haven't seen you all day."

"I've been busy."

"Any new info on the missing artwork?" Danielle asked.

"Yeah. Annette helped with a little undercover operation and we're back to square one. Every single person who works in the gallery is a suspect."

Millie paused as a group of guests approached, asking if the buffet was open. "The buffet is closed for another half an hour, but you can still grab some pizza or sandwiches from the deli in the back."

Half an hour before the ship was scheduled to pull up anchor, Millie wandered over to check with

Suharto to find out how many passengers still hadn't returned to the ship. They were down to a handful and Millie resumed her spot next to Danielle when a commotion near the scanning machines caught their attention.

"Get your hands off me!" a woman shrieked. Millie shifted to the side for a better look. It was Danvers' girlfriend, Brigitte.

Chapter 17

Brigitte swatted at one of the ship's security guards. "You can't stop me from bringing this on board. What is this? A prison?"

"Now Brigitte." Ted Danvers attempted to calm the woman. "You don't have to raise your voice."

"Don't shush me," she screeched. The woman clutched tightly to the bag she was carrying. "You are not going to scan this bag." She stomped through security's walk through metal detector.

Beep. Beep.

Thankfully, Oscar, one of the security supervisors, was on hand and he strode over to Brigitte. "We must search the bag."

Millie held her breath as the two of them glared at each other.

"Give the man the bag," Danvers said in a low voice.

Brigitte shot Danvers a dirty look and reluctantly handed Oscar the shopping bag.

Oscar calmly walked to the scanning equipment. He glanced inside the bag before placing it on the moving conveyor belt. After the package cleared the scanner, Brigitte snatched it off the belt. "I hope you're happy," she snarled and then marched to the bank of elevators.

Ted Danvers hurried after her, barely making it inside before the doors closed.

"Wait here," Millie told Danielle before jogging to the scanning machine and Oscar's side. "What was in the bag?"

"Furry pink handcuffs and maracas," Oscar whispered.

"Maracas?"

"Yes. Maracas. Shake, shake, shake."

"Oh my," Millie grinned. "To each his own, I guess."

Brigitte's meltdown was the highlight – or lowlight – of the afternoon boarding, and when the ship set sail from St. Thomas, Millie let out a sigh of relief. She had officially survived the first half of the week.

Wednesday's itinerary was a full day at sea and Millie had an action-packed schedule planned, starting with a goofy mini-golf tournament, followed by a painting party and then a cupcake-decorating contest. There was even a digital camera seminar.

Millie swung by the specialty coffee shop and splurged on a large iced mochaccino. She settled into a bistro chair, slipped her reading glasses on and sipped the chocolatey caffeine as she studied the day's *Cruise Ship Chronicles*.

Julio Marchan, the ship's magician, was scheduled to perform two shows that evening before he jumped ship in St. Croix.

After going over the schedule, she headed back to her cabin to take a brief break. The room was dark and quiet.

Millie eased onto the edge of her bunk, but the temptation to curl up and take a quick nap was too tempting so she sat at the small desk instead, kicked off her shoes and began rubbing her aching feet.

Her mind wandered to the Danvers family. Josh mentioned he thought Danvers wasn't that bad and it was Brigitte who was behind a lot of the issues that arose. After Brigitte's meltdown earlier, Millie believed it.

Then there was poor Teddy. How could Danvers not see that his son was crying out for attention? What would happen if Danvers proposed and he and Brigitte married? She wondered if there was still such a thing as boarding schools.

Millie freshened up, slipped her shoes back on and headed out. She stopped by Patterson's office to see if he had any new leads in the art heist, but his office was dark. Millie's next stop was deck ten.

She caught a glimpse of a security guard standing sentinel at the end of the hallway leading to the grand suite and Millie wondered if Teddy was still inside.

At the other end of the hall, she ran into her friend, Brody, who had recently been promoted to the head of night security. She glanced at her watch. "It's the middle of the afternoon. What are you doing up here?"

"Working."

"I know that. Did Patterson move you to the day shift?"

"Temporarily." Brody shrugged. "Danvers insists that a security supervisor be stationed outside his suite so here I am."

"That's crazy."

"Yep." Brody glanced over Millie's shoulder and lowered his voice. "The woman, Brigitte? She's crazy." He twirled his finger next to his temple. "Kimel Pang is cleaning their room and is only allowed inside under the direct supervision of Brigitte. Teddy has been in the suite all day."

"Teddy is grounded," Millie said. "Did you say Kimel Pang is cleaning their suite? Isn't he the head of housekeeping?"

"Yeah and he's none too happy about it. He says the woman follows him around, watching him like a hawk, like she thinks he's going to steal something."

"So how long are you going to be here?" Millie motioned toward the suite.

"Until the Danvers leave the ship on Saturday. At least they don't spend a lot of time up here. They order room service for breakfast each morning. 8:00 a.m. sharp. I don't see 'em much during the day but evenings are like clockwork. They head down for dinner at 7:00 and then Brigitte returns to the suite while Mr. Danvers spends the rest of the evening in the casino. I knock off at midnight so I'm not sure what time he returns." Brody changed the subject. "How're you doing this week with Andy gone?"

"So far so good except, for some missing artwork. The art gallery manager seems to think Andy and/or I had something to do with that."

"What are you gonna do with a bunch of art?" Brody asked.

"Good question," Millie said. "I guess I better get going. Keep up the good work." She patted Brody's arm and headed up the steps. The Danvers' unplanned visit had definitely upset the apple cart. At least there was light at the end of the tunnel and only a few more days left.

***

"Someone ought to put their foot down," Danielle said, after Millie told her Danvers insisted on having a security supervisor guard their hall and the head of housekeeping was cleaning the Danvers' suite.

"Who?"

"Captain Armati. I mean, he is captain of this ship," Danielle pointed out.

"And Danvers could have Captain Armati fired. Don't forget we're trying to get his approval to wed and stay on board Siren of the Seas."

"True. I heard someone say Danvers and Brigitte aren't even engaged."

"I heard the same thing," Millie said.

"While you're here..." Danielle grasped Millie's arm and pulled her off to the side. "I know it's kind of short notice, but I was wondering if I could have a couple of hours off on Thursday while we're in St. Croix."

"Of course." Danielle rarely asked for time off and Millie's interest was piqued. "Are you doing something special?"

Danielle wrinkled her nose. "Sorta. I'm going on a private island tour of Fort Christiansvaern, and then touring a botanical garden. I think we're also stopping off at Rhythms and Rainbows beach before heading back to the ship. I'll probably be gone about four hours, but if it's a problem…"

Millie cut her off. "It's not a problem. If you can hang around until the first wave of passengers head out for the day, you're free to go do whatever. So who is 'we'?"

The pink in Danielle's cheeks deepened.

"Spill the beans," Millie said.

"I have a date; I mean a non-date with Stephen Chow."

"You're going out with the ship's acupuncturist?" Millie remembered the time Andy had sent her to Chow's office on a recon mission. The man had stabbed her with what felt like a thousand needles. After the painful experience, she vowed never to let Andy talk her into something like that again.

"Yeah. I've been in there a couple times, trying to alleviate my anxiety and work on getting rid of my nightmares." Danielle had experienced nightmares off and on since she'd moved in with Millie.

The nightmares were linked to the death of Danielle's brother, Casey. The young woman had once admitted to Millie she'd been with Casey when he died and it haunted her.

"Is it working?"

"I think so." Danielle nodded. "We've kind of gotten to know each other during my visits and yesterday he asked if I would like to join him for a tour of the island."

Millie's assistant had very few friends on board the ship and she'd only shown a passing interest in one or two of the male crewmembers. "I hope you have a great time. C'mon." She tugged on the young woman's arm. "I think it's time to go home."

By the time Millie got ready for bed, she could barely keep her eyes open and as soon as her head hit the pillow, she was out like a light.

Despite being exhausted, Millie woke early the next morning, ready for a full day at sea. She'd scheduled a mid-morning meeting with some of the staff since they'd officially made it halfway through the cruise and she wanted to stay on top of any concerns or problems.

After the meeting ended, Millie made her way upstairs where she ran into Josh in front of the library. "Just the person I was looking for." He pointed at Millie's radio. "I've been trying to reach you."

Millie glanced down. "I was in a meeting and turned the volume down." She fiddled with the dial. "Try it now."

Josh pressed the talk button on the side of his radio. "Millie. Do you copy?"

"Go ahead Josh."

"Can you meet me in front of the library?"

"10-4."

Millie clipped the walkie-talkie to her belt. "How is Teddy?"

"Sick."

"He's sick?" Millie asked.

"Yeah. I went up there at ten this morning. He was white as a ghost when he answered the door and told me he's been throwing up."

"Oh dear. I wonder if he ate something bad?" She hoped not. The last thing they needed was for Danvers to start criticizing the ship's food.

"He said since he was grounded all last night, Brigitte and his dad brought him some food from upstairs and he got sick after eating it."

"What did he eat?"

"I didn't ask." Josh shook his head. "I did ask him why he didn't order room service and he said the food on the room service menu was gross."

Millie knew she should check to find out what Teddy had eaten and to make sure no one else had gotten sick, but the last thing she wanted to do was knock on the Danvers' door and ask.

"I told him I would check back after lunch to see if he was feeling better."

"Was Teddy alone?"

"Yeah. I didn't see Mr. Danvers or Brigitte." Millie thanked him for the information, assigned him a couple of events to co-host and then headed to the galley. Perhaps Annette had heard if others on board the ship had become ill the previous day.

Millie found her friend hunched over a large pot stirring soup stock. "You should move a cot into the kitchen."

"No kidding. How's the investigation going?" Annette asked.

"It's on the backburner. I've got my hands full."

"Don't we all? What's up? You normally don't pop in just to say 'hi' this time of the day."

"Josh Appleton told me Teddy Danvers became ill after eating some food Brigitte and his dad

229

brought to the room last night. Have you heard any other complaints?"

"Not a peep." Annette shook her head. "Are you sure he's not faking it?"

"Josh said he was pale and looked ill so I don't think so." Millie went on to tell Annette how the Danvers insisted that a security supervisor guard their floor and how Kimel Pang, the housekeeping supervisor, was cleaning their suite.

Annette burst out laughing. "Man, I wish I was a fly on the wall to watch Kimel clean the suite. I don't think he's touched a toilet bowl brush in twenty years." She swiped at her eyes. "That is the funniest thing I've heard all day."

"Danielle has a date," Millie said.

Annette stopped laughing and her expression grew serious. "Our little Danielle is going out on a date?"

"You're never in a million years gonna guess who it's with."

"Donovan."

"Nope." Millie shook her head. "You know he has a thing for one of the dancers."

"No, I didn't." Annette leaned forward. "Which one?"

"All of them," Millie teased.

"That's not fair," Annette waved her spoon at Millie. "At least tell me who Danielle is going out with."

"Stephen Chow."

"The acupuncturist?" Annette's eyes widened. "Seriously?"

"Yep. They're going on a private tour in St. Croix."

"Well, I'll be. I never would've guessed."

The women chatted for a few more minutes before Millie exited the galley. She made her rounds from the top of the ship to the bottom and waited until early afternoon to call Josh. "Josh, do you copy?"

"Go ahead Millie."

"Can you meet me near the galley side door?"

Josh told her he would and then showed up a few minutes later. "How is Teddy?"

"Still sick." Josh shook his head. "Poor guy looks terrible. I'm beginning to think it's not a bad batch of food."

Millie was, too. Josh promised to check on him again and Millie made a beeline for the medical center.

Doctor Gundervan was in and told Millie he hadn't heard that Teddy was ill.

Millie thanked the doctor, exited his office and slowly wandered down the hall. She stopped abruptly when a horrible thought crossed her mind. What if someone on board the ship had intentionally made Teddy ill?

Chapter 18

Ocean Treasures gift shop was full of shoppers so Millie stepped to the back and examined a display of souvenir spoons as she waited for the crowd to thin.

"Enjoy your day." Cat smiled as she dropped the receipt inside the store bag and handed it to the last customer in line. She waited until the couple exited the store and then wandered over to the spoon display. "You look like you're ready to explode."

"I need your help. I need to find out if anyone who is staying in the grand suite purchased merchandise from the store."

"That should be easy. Do you know the cabin number?"

"No. Hang on." Millie unclipped her radio. "Brody, do you copy?"

"Go ahead Millie."

"Call me on channel 150." Channel 150 was a channel Millie used only when she didn't want everyone else with a walkie-talkie to listen to her conversation. Like now.

"10-4."

Her radio squawked again. "What's up?"

"I need the cabin number."

"Why do you need my cabin number?" Brody asked.

"Let me rephrase that. I need the Danvers' cabin number."

"Oh. It's 10220."

"Perfect." Millie jotted the number on a piece of paper. "Thanks."

"What are you up to?"

"Just working on a little research, Brody. Talk to you later." Millie quickly switched back to the regular broadcast channel before he could ask more questions.

Cat stepped over to the computer and tapped on the keyboard. "10220." She scanned the screen. "Nothing. They haven't purchased a single item."

"Just my luck." Millie drummed her fingers on the countertop. "I need Brigitte, Danvers' girlfriend's last name."

"I thought they were married."

"Nope. Not even engaged."

"So you're going to spy on her?"

"Spy is a strong word. I want to do a little research," Millie said.

"Are you crazy? If Danvers finds out you're snooping on his girlfriend, he'll fire you."

"I have to - for Teddy's sake." Millie shared her suspicions, how he'd been grounded and then became ill; yet, as far as she could tell, no one else on board had complained. "I checked with your beau, Doctor Gundervan, and the family hasn't visited the clinic to have Teddy checked out."

"Maybe he's having an allergic reaction," Cat said.

"Or food poisoning," Millie said. "If I can figure out Brigitte's last name, I can do a little online research."

"Josh is in constant contact with the family. Do you think there's a way for him to perhaps get a sample of Teddy's food to send in for testing?"

"Excellent idea, but it's flawed. Say we were able to get a food sample, by the time we got the results back, Teddy could be dead," Millie said.

"I have an idea," Cat said. "Describe Brigitte."

"She's a petite, pretty blonde." Millie thought of the designer suit Annette had borrowed. "She wears designer clothes."

"Does she wear a lot of jewelry?"

"Hmm." Millie had only seen the woman a few times in passing. "I'm sure she does. Why?"

A slow smile crept across Cat's face. "I have an idea. What if *Ocean Treasures* held an exclusive, by invitation-only jewelry sale? A sale so exclusive; we're only going to invite one person?"

"Brigitte?"

"Bingo." Cat hurried on. "We'll have to plan it for after hours and keep it on the down low. We can do it tonight, after the store closes. If we can lure Brigitte in here to purchase something...voila! We'll have her last name."

Millie thought of her recent conversation with Brody, how after dinner Danvers headed to the casino for the rest of the evening while Brigitte returned to the suite. "I have an idea. Actually, I have the perfect idea." She stared out the window, deep in thought. "What kind of unbelievable sale could you offer which would entice Brigitte to actually purchase something?"

"I don't know. I hadn't thought that far ahead." Cat frowned. "I could do what every other retailer does and tweak some of the tags, bumping the price up and then red-line slashing so it *looks* like a great bargain."

"But it's the same price?" Millie asked.

"Yeah, I mean. It would only be for a couple of hours and then I would change the prices back."

"It might work," Millie said. "But we need other shoppers so it doesn't look suspicious."

"I'm sure I could talk my cabin mate, Lila, into coming up here, pretending to be one of my invitation-only shoppers."

With a simple plan in place, Millie's next step was to create, print and slip a special announcement under the Danvers' cabin door.

She headed to the office computer and printer area, the same area where Millie printed out the *Cruise Ship Chronicles*. Thankfully, no one was in the back and it only took her a few moments to find a blank invitation and envelope.

Millie had printed personalized invitations before, thanks to Andy, who hosted an array of exclusive, invitation-only past guest parties with Captain Armati.

She printed the envelope first, "Special Guests – Suite 10220." Millie needed something that would knock Brigitte's socks off...an offer she couldn't resist. "I've got it," she whispered under her breath. When she finished printing the invitation, she held it up for inspection:

"By Invitation Only!

You have been hand-selected to join us in the Ocean Treasures Gift shop for an exclusive one-of-a-kind jewelry sale. Don't miss out on this fabulous gold, diamond and precious gem extravaganza.

For one hour only – 9:30 p.m. – 10:30 p.m. this evening, we will be hosting our premier blowout sale with unbelievable prices on an array of dazzling gems.

*Complimentary champagne available."

Millie didn't know what else to say and hoped the invitation would be enough to entice Brigitte to visit the store and buy something.

She carefully slid the invitation inside the envelope and slipped both into her pocket before exiting the copy room and heading to deck ten. With a quick glance in both directions, she hurried to the hallway where the grand suite was located.

Her heart sank when she spied Brody standing guard.

Millie cleared her throat and smiled. "Hi Brody." She started to pass by when Brody stuck his arm out, almost clotheslining her. "What are you up to now?"

"Me?" Millie widened her eyes innocently.

"Yeah. You look guilty as all get-out."

"I'm simply dropping off an invitation for Brigitte."

"What kind of invitation?"

"Aren't you going a little overboard with this gatekeeper gig?" Millie teased.

"No. Part of my job is to find out who is in this area and why."

"I already told you," Millie said. "I'm dropping off an invitation. It's to a jewelry sale, if you must know."

"Okay."

Millie could feel the heat of Brody's stare creep up her neck as she walked down the hall. When she reached Danvers' suite, she bent down and shoved the invitation under the door before retracing her steps.

"Why didn't you just drop it in the message bin next to the door?" Brody asked.

"Because I want to make sure Brigitte sees the invitation. What is this...50 questions?"

"No. Five questions and I've got one left," Brody said.

Annoyed, Millie wrinkled her nose. "What's that?"

"Can you stand guard for a couple of minutes? I gotta use the restroom."

"Of course." Millie said. "Take your time."

Brody thanked Millie before rounding the corner and heading to the bank of nearby elevators. She glanced behind her to make sure no one was in the hall before slowly walking to the Danvers suite. She tapped lightly and then a second time.

No one answered and Millie took it as a positive sign. Perhaps Teddy was feeling better and wasn't cooped up inside. She made her way back to Brody's post and he returned a short time later.

"Thanks Millie," Brody said. He reached for a clipboard hanging on the wall. "I'm still gonna have to log your visit."

"You have to log visits?"

"Yep. I write down the name of every person who enters this hall. Danvers' rules, not mine."

"That's ridiculous," Millie said.

"I agree, but I'm not the one making the rules."
He jotted Millie's name on the log and then hung
the clipboard back on the hook.

Brody thanked Millie again, before she wandered
out of the suite area and to the ship's galley. Now
all she had to do was track down a bottle of
champagne and some glasses.

***

Millie spent the afternoon darting from stem to
stern and top to bottom. It was a busy afternoon
and the day flew by. Thankfully, she didn't have
time to dwell on the invitation-only shopping
event. The last thing Millie wanted to do was to
get Cat in trouble.

She hoped that wouldn't happen, although not a
single one of Millie's investigations had ever gone
off without a hitch.

Technically, it wasn't an investigation, but more
of a fact-finding exercise. Millie needed Brigitte's

last name and the only way to do that was ask Donovan for a copy of the master guest list. Donovan would ask why and her answer would raise all sorts of questions Millie wasn't ready to answer.

By the time 9:00 p.m. rolled around, Millie had almost convinced herself the plan was flawless and that nothing would go wrong. Almost.

Chapter 19

At 9:06 p.m., Cat Wellington locked the store doors behind her last customer. She turned the window sign to "Closed" and hurried to the back where the jewelry display cases were located.

Her hands shook as she unlocked the cabinet and carefully removed a tray of rings. Earlier, when she hadn't been helping customers, Cat had created a new set of price tags for the high-end jewelry items.

Her strategy was to create tags 25% higher than the current prices and then slash the price, giving the appearance the buyer would be getting a great deal on the jewelry when, in fact, they would be paying regular price.

To entice Brigitte to purchase something, Cat decided to throw in her own employee discount.

Last, but not least, she was able to persuade her cabin mate, Lila, to show up, posing as a shopper.

Since Lila worked in the employee lounge and kitchen areas, Cat was certain Brigitte and Lila had never crossed paths.

Lila showed up at 9:09 on the dot. Cat unlocked the door and motioned her inside.

"Do I look okay?" Lila stepped inside the store and tugged on the collar of her blouse.

"Yes. It's perfect," Cat said. "All you have to do is pretend to be shopping." She pointed at the young woman's gray capris slacks and cotton candy pink button down blouse. "I may have to borrow your outfit someday."

A nervous Lila nodded. "You're still gonna owe me one."

"I promise I'll clean the bathroom for the next week."

"Be my guest." Lila relaxed her stiff stance as she looked around. "Do I have to buy something?"

"No. You can peruse the jewelry trays and then say something like you have to ask your husband. Here." Cat thrust a fluted glass, filled with a golden liquid, into Lila's hand. "Have a glass of champagne."

"I can do that." Lila sipped the bubbly and wandered over to the jewelry display.

At 9:45, Cat was beginning to suspect Brigitte would be a no-show. By 9:55, she was certain Brigitte wasn't going to show and was contemplating calling Millie to give her an update when a petite blonde woman materialized. She stood in front of the door, waving a printed envelope.

Cat hurried to unlock the door and motioned the woman inside.

"Invitation only?"

"Yes." Cat took the invitation and glanced at the front of the envelope. "I'm glad you could make it..." She lifted her brow.

"Brigitte."

"Brigitte." Cat smiled warmly.

Lila looked up from the display case and gave Brigitte a small nod before resuming her perusal of the goods.

"I don't have much time."

"Of course," Cat said smoothly. "Champagne?" She grabbed a glass and handed it to the woman. "Let me show you our best deals." She motioned Brigitte to the display cases in the back and pulled out a tray of the gems with the stickers she'd just replaced.

Brigitte shifted the champagne glass to her other hand and plucked an oval sapphire ring from the tray. She gazed at the ring and then flipped the tag to check the price. "This ring costs three-thousand, five-hundred dollars?"

"It's been marked down," Cat pointed out.

"Huh." Brigitte placed the ring back inside the tray and reached for a square cut emerald ring. It was one of Cat's favorite pieces.

Brigitte didn't bother checking the price and slipped the ring on her finger. She tilted her hand and then held it up to the light.

"It's a magnificent piece," Cat said.

The woman removed the ring and studied the price tag before handing it to Cat. "Four-thousand, six-hundred fifty."

"You have discriminating taste," Cat replied. "It's on sale."

"I see."

Lila slipped in next to Brigitte. "It is a beautiful ring." She motioned to the ring. "Do you mind if I try it on?"

"Of course not," Cat smiled and handed Lila the ring.

Lila wiggled the ring onto her finger. "It's gorgeous." She flipped the tag over. "The price seems reasonable. I have to run it by my Bertrand first."

Brigitte's eyes narrowed. "I saw it first."

"I saw it second." Lila handed the ring to Cat, who placed it back inside the tray before sliding the entire tray inside the display case and locking it.

"Let me track down Bertrand." Lila hurried to the door and Cat trailed behind, unlocking the door for her. "Bertrand?" she whispered under her breath.

Lila winked at Cat before marching off.

"Can I show you anything else?" Cat asked when she returned to the jewelry case.

"No. I think I've seen enough." Brigitte slipped her tote bag off her shoulder and reached inside. "I would like to return a piece of costume jewelry I purchased a few weeks ago while I was on the Baroness of the Seas."

Brigitte pulled out a Majestic Cruise Lines shopping bag and handed it to Cat. "One of the stones in the necklace already fell out."

"I'm sorry to hear that." Cat reached inside the bag and pulled out the sales receipt. "As long as it was within the last 90 days, I can give you a full refund."

Cat's mind raced as she carried the bag and receipt to the cash register. Brigitte was going to slip away without Cat finding out the woman's last name.

Think fast, Cat. She reached for the computer's mouse when a brilliant idea popped into her head. "Would you like to replace it with another piece?"

"No." Brigitte shook her head. "It's a piece of junk."

"I see." Cat began tapping the keys. "All I need is your first and last name to complete the refund."

"Whatever for?' Brigitte waved her hand. "You have the receipt and the merchandise. I've never heard of such a thing."

"It's a new company policy," Cat fibbed. "And it's only required on jewelry purchases since we return the defective merchandise to the manufacturer."

"Fine." Brigitte crossed her arms. "Brigitte Perez."

Cat couldn't help herself. Her eyes wandered to the woman's platinum blonde hair.

Brigitte patted her hair. "Blondes have more fun."

"So I've heard." Cat completed the transaction, opened the cash register and counted out one-hundred, fourteen dollars and twelve cents. "How does the Baroness of the Seas compare to the Siren of the Seas?"

Brigitte took the money and slipped it into her purse. "The ships are similar in many ways. The counters in the suite bathroom on the Baroness are slightly larger, as is the balcony. Room service on Baroness is a little slower, but the dining room service is more attentive." The woman rambled on as she compared the two ships and Cat was beginning to regret asking.

"It sounds as if you cruise a lot." Cat walked Brigitte to the door and unlocked it. "I'm sorry we weren't able to find the perfect jewelry piece to compliment your collection. If you decide you would like to purchase the emerald, I'll honor the price as long as I still have it on hand and no one else purchases it."

"Why can't you hold it for me, at least until tomorrow?"

Cat wrinkled her brow. "Well...okay. I'll hold it for you until I open the store tomorrow morning." She thanked the woman for participating in the "special event" and waited until Brigitte was out of sight before locking the door. She quickly swapped the tags, checked to make sure she'd secured all of the jewelry cases and then shut the store lights off before hurrying out of the store.

It was time to track down Millie and Annette, who were waiting for her inside the kitchen galley.

***

 "So you're saying Brigitte was on the Baroness of the Seas a few weeks ago?" Millie asked.

"Yep." Cat nodded. "She returned a piece of costume jewelry and I specifically asked her about the other ship." She went on to tell them how she managed to get Brigitte's last name by telling her it was required on all jewelry returns.

"Very clever," Annette complimented. "So what's her last name?"

"Perez."

"Brigitte Perez?" Millie wrinkled her nose. "She doesn't look like a 'Perez,' not that I'm stereotyping, but I don't know many women named Perez with blonde hair."

"Bottle," Annette said. "I pegged it right from the get-go."

"It's an uncommon combination of names," Millie said. "I wish I had a computer."

Annette held up her index finger. "Your wish is my command." She reached inside one of the galley cabinets and pulled out a laptop. "I figured we might need this." She flipped the top up and began tapping the keys. "Danvers is from Florida, so I guess it would be safe to assume Brigitte is also from Florida."

"Yep." Millie leaned forward on her elbows. "B-R-I-G-I-T-T-E."

"Got it," Annette said. "I think I might've found something." She squinted her eyes and studied the screen. "It's a short news article in the *Miami Herald* about Danvers. Brigitte is in the picture with him."

Millie hurried to the other side of the counter and peered over Annette's shoulder. "What does it say?"

"She previously worked at The Turquoise Isle Gentlemen's Club."

"She's a stripper?" Cat asked.

"Was. It looks like she gave up the position for a more lucrative venture," Annette said.

"Hooking up with Ted Danvers doesn't make her a criminal," Millie pointed out. "Opportunist? Probably. Criminal? No. Is there anything else?"

"Nope. It was a small blurb." Annette said. "From what we know of Danvers, my guess is he contacted the newspaper and threatened to sue them if they printed anything else about his girlfriend."

"Ugh." Millie clenched her fists. "There has to be something else."

"There is. We can check to see if she has a rap sheet." Annette shifted her gaze to the screen.

"You can find that out?"

"Sure. All you gotta do is search the public records database. What county is Miami in?"

"Miami-Dade," Millie and Cat said in unison.

Annette leaned back. "Well, lookee here."

Chapter 20

"Check it out." Annette jabbed her finger at the screen. "Brigitte was charged with misdemeanor shoplifting back in 2015."

"Oh no," Cat groaned. "I didn't keep that close of an eye on her. I hope she didn't steal anything from the store."

Millie remembered Donovan telling her Danvers and Brigitte toured the ship the night before it set sail. It was at that time Danvers informed Donovan he and his family planned to cruise that week. "Danvers and Brigitte toured the ship Friday night."

She began to pace. "According to Brenda, this was right around the time the first piece of art went missing."

"Interesting," Annette said. "She also goes by the name Brigitte Perez Bealitz, which is an unusual combination. Let's see if we get a hit on that combo." She tapped the keyboard and then clicked the mouse. "Jackpot!"

"What does it say?" Millie had forgotten her glasses and the words on the screen were blurred.

"Oh goodness," Cat whispered. "You're not gonna like this Millie."

"Like what?"

"Brigitte was arrested in 2014 for suspicion of murder of her late husband, entrepreneur, Eduardo Bealitz," Annette said. "The charges were eventually dropped."

"Did they state the cause of death?" Millie asked.

"Inconclusive and Ms. Perez Bealitz had her husband's remains cremated the day the authorities released the body," Annette said.

"Why did they suspect her of murdering her husband?" Cat asked.

"It says here, based on information provided by Mr. Bealitz's relatives, the local authorities were working on opening a new investigation and were in the process of filing papers to block his cremation, but it was too late. No body. No evidence. No crime." Annette shifted her feet. "They interviewed Mr. Bealitz's daughter and she claims her father was complaining of not feeling well and had been bed-ridden for several days prior to his death."

"Let me guess. She suspected her father had been poisoned." Millie's stomach churned. What if the daughter's suspicions had been correct and Brigitte had poisoned her husband? Was Teddy next?

The color drained from Millie's face. "We have to do something." She fumbled with her radio. "I have to talk to Josh. We mustn't let the woman near Teddy again."

"But how can we stop her?' Cat asked. "We have no proof."

"Even if we're able to get a sample of the food Teddy is eating, it will take days to get it to a lab and for them to return the results," Annette pointed out.

Millie pressed the button on her radio. "Josh, do you copy?"

"Go ahead Millie."

"I'd like to chat with you if you have a moment. Where are you?"

"In the crew lounge."

"I'll be right there." Millie clipped the radio to her belt. "I need Josh to find out from Teddy what he ate, when he first started feeling ill and if both Ted Danvers and Brigitte brought him his food."

Annette shut the lid on the computer. "You better be careful, Millie. Accusing Danvers' girlfriend of poisoning his son is a serious accusation."

"I know, but what other choice do I have? I can't stand by and let Brigitte kill him."

"Not that you'd ever do this, Millie, but don't jump to conclusions. It could be he did eat something bad. I would talk to Josh first, before you do anything else," Cat wisely advised.

"Okay. I'll wait to see what Josh has to say," Millie promised. "I better get going." She thanked Cat and Annette for helping her and exited the galley.

Josh was waiting near the bar when Millie arrived. He moved to the next seat to make room. "You sound like you need to talk. What's up?"

"It's about Teddy." Millie climbed onto the barstool. "Did you see him at all today?"

"Yep." Josh nodded. "We spent a couple hours together this evening. He seems to have completely recovered from whatever was ailing him. We're going to hang out tomorrow while his father and Brigitte go ashore for some sort of local food tasting and port shopping."

"I'm so glad Teddy is feeling better," Millie said. "Do you know what time they're leaving?"

Josh stared over Millie's head. "I think around nine or so. I'm going to swing by there around ten o'clock, after they leave."

"Have you ever been inside the Danvers' suite?"

"Nope." Josh shook his head. "He's usually in the hall waiting for me, except for when he was sick and I met him at the door. It's kind of weird."

"Unless you're hiding something," Millie muttered under her breath. "So what are you and Teddy planning to do tomorrow?"

"I promised him I'd give him a tour of the backstage, the main theater's sound booth. He also wants to see where I live and what my cabin looks like. Why?"

"Mmm...no particular reason. Can you do me a huge favor?"

"Sure, but then you'll owe me two."

"Two it is," Millie agreed. "Can you make sure you don't bring Teddy back to the suite until at least noon?"

"Okay. That shouldn't be a problem." Josh glanced around and leaned forward. "You're going to search their suite, aren't you?"

Millie met his gaze. "Do you really want to know?"

"No." Josh smiled. "Ignorance is bliss."

"Do you think it's possible someone inside the Danvers' suite is trying to poison Teddy?"

"I hadn't thought of that," Josh said. "Is that what you think?"

"I don't know what to think." Millie slid off the stool and patted her radio. "If anything changes, please radio me before you bring Teddy back to the suite."

"Will do." Josh lifted his hand in a mock salute. "Good luck."

"Thanks." Millie stood. "I'm gonna need it."

Millie made her final rounds and finished near the Sky Chapel. The stress of the day's events had taken its toll. She was mentally and physically

264

exhausted, but instead of heading to her cabin, she tiptoed inside.

The only light was the glow coming from the cross, which hung on the front wall of the chapel. Millie slowly walked down the center aisle and perched on the edge of the front row pew. She clasped her hands together and gazed at the cross that meant so much to her.

Millie's chapel attendance had slipped lately. She'd gotten so caught up in trying to find a way for her and Nic to marry, not to mention staying on top of everything during Andy's absence, she barely had time to breathe. Luke 12:29 popped into her head:

"And do not set your heart on what you will eat or drink; do not worry about it. For the pagan world runs after all such things, and your Father knows that you need them. But seek his kingdom, and these things will be given to you as well." Luke 12:29-31 NIV.

A wave of guilt washed over her as it dawned on her she'd been razor-focused on her life, her job and her own problems. She closed her eyes and prayed God would give her peace, that he would show her how to help young Teddy and help her find a way that Nic and she could have their "happily ever after."

She also thought of Josh and his mother. There had to be a way to help them raise the money for the clinical trials in Texas.

Perhaps she was trying too hard to solve all of life's problems on her own. "Lord, please help me. You know what I'm facing. You know my worries. Thank you for your son, my Savior, Jesus. Amen."

Millie wiggled off the bench and as she made her way out of the dark chapel, it felt as if a huge weight had been lifted from her shoulders.

By the time Millie reached the cabin, Danielle was already in bed and fast asleep. The young woman had stepped up to the plate. She'd gone above and beyond her job and Millie vowed not to forget it.

She changed into her pajamas, scrubbed her face and brushed her teeth before slipping out of the bathroom and crawling into her bunk. She folded her hands, closed her eyes and then prayed for her family in Michigan, for her cruise ship family, for Teddy and the Danvers family.

She slept through the night and never stirred until Danielle gently shook her arm.

Millie opened one eye and gazed at the young woman standing over her. "What time is it?" she croaked.

"Time to get up," Danielle said. "I let you sleep as long as I could, but if we don't grab a bite to eat, we'll have to go straight to the gangway."

Millie flung her covers back and squinted at the bedside clock. "Oh my gosh. It's 6:30." She scrambled out of her bunk and strode to the bathroom. "I'll be right out," she said before closing the door.

Millie yanked her clothes on, brushed her teeth and fixed her hair in record time before emerging from the bathroom.

"You weren't kidding," Danielle said. "I think you set a new world record for getting ready."

"I can't believe I slept through your alarm," Millie said as she slipped into her work shoes.

"You didn't. I woke up before it went off." Danielle grinned. "You were in your bunk sawing logs."

"Don't laugh too hard. You do the same thing." Millie patted Danielle's arm and then opened the cabin door. "We're in the home stretch now. Only two more days."

"Forty-nine hours and ten minutes," Danielle said. "But who's counting?"

The crew mess was exactly that...a mess. A long line extended down the side, out the door and into the hall.

"We're never gonna make it in time," Danielle groaned. "There's Nikki near the front." She cupped her hands to her lips. "Hey Nikki, grab a couple extra breakfast sandwiches."

Nikki gave Danielle a thumbs-up and the women stepped out of the line and headed to the coffee station. They each poured a cup and met Nikki near the long counter in the back.

"Thanks. We're on a tight schedule this morning." Danielle took two of the breakfast sandwiches and handed one to Millie.

"Aren't we all?" Nikki rolled her eyes. "This has been one of the longest weeks ever." Nikki told them there was a large group of travel agents on board, checking out the ship's new upgrades and were nitpicking every little thing.

"Are they complaining about the activities?" Millie asked as she bit into her sandwich.

"Nope. Just their rooms, the water pressure, the food, the drink prices," Nikki said.

"Now that is a legitimate complaint," Danielle said.

Cruise ships were notorious for inflating not only the price of soda and water, but also other drinks and specialty coffees.

Millie polished off the rest of her sandwich and downed the last of her coffee before hopping off the barstool. "I better head up to the gangway."

"I'm right behind you," Danielle mumbled.

"Take your time," Millie said. She thanked Nikki for grabbing their sandwiches and wished her a stress-free day before heading out of the crew dining room.

When she reached the exit, the atrium was already packed with passengers waiting for the ship to clear customs so they could disembark.

St. Croix was one of the quieter islands and boasted a beautiful beach area close to the port.

Captain Armati and she had spent a few hours on shore, but never in the beach area, preferring instead to find secluded, quiet spots away from the crowds. Although Millie enjoyed all that St. Croix had to offer, she was looking forward to visiting new ports.

Danielle joined her just in time for the all-clear signal and the guests to begin departing the ship. "What time is your hot date with Doc Chow?"

"It's not a hot date," Danielle insisted. "It's a non-hot date."

"Okay. What time are you and Doctor Chow heading out?"

"Ten, but I can change it if you want me to," Danielle quickly added.

"No. I don't want you to change it," Millie said. "With this many guests getting off already, I think it will die down around 9:30 so you can go get ready and be back here by ten."

"Thanks Millie. I appreciate it."

"Thank you, Danielle. You're been a huge help this week." A guest approached to ask a question and the women returned to the task at hand.

When 9:30 rolled around and the crowds thinned, Danielle left, returning a short time later with a man Millie barely recognized as the acupuncturist who had tortured her with a thousand burning needles.

"Have fun," Millie told them and then glanced at her watch. It was just after ten. Millie knew Ted Danvers and Brigitte had already exited the ship. She'd watched them make their way down the gangway.

Millie hadn't heard from Josh so she assumed Teddy and he were together and the grand suite was now empty. Her heart skipped a beat as she started up the stairs to deck ten. It was now or never. Tomorrow was the last day, a day at sea with all passengers, including the Danvers, on board. If she followed through with her plan to snoop inside the Danvers' suite, this would be her only chance.

Thankfully, Brody was standing guard at one end of the hallway. He raised a brow when he saw Millie approached. "Hey Millie. What's up?"

"I need a favor," she said bluntly. "I need you to take a walk around the corner and come back in about ten minutes."

"Why?" Brody asked.

"Because you owe me one."

"Tell me you're not going into the Danvers' suite."

"I'm not going into the Danvers' suite," Millie said. "Now beat it."

"I hope you know what you're doing." Brody shook his head before walking away and disappearing around the corner.

Millie waited until he was out of sight before jogging down the hall to suite 10220. She lifted her lanyard from around her neck, slipped her keycard into the door slot and silently pushed the door open.

Chapter 21

Millie closed the cabin door, reached inside her front pocket and pulled out a small flashlight. She slid the closet door open and beamed the light along the closet shelves, which were filled with clothing, socks and underwear.

She juggled the flashlight in one hand and bounced on her tiptoes as she ran her hand along the top shelf.

Her fingers grasped the plastic buckle of one of the ship's life jackets, the only thing that was on the shelf.

Millie slid the closet door to the other side and beamed the light inside. The closet was filled with an assortment of dress clothes. Dress shoes lined the bottom of the closet. She eased the door shut and crept to the make-up counter where she searched the cabinet drawers.

Next, she moved onto the adjoining bathroom and ended her search by looking under the bed. There was no hidden artwork inside the grand suite. Millie was beginning to suspect her hunch was all wrong, that Brigitte wasn't the art thief but merely a petty thief.

She made her way to the door, gently pulled it open and stuck her head into the hall. She looked both ways before slipping out of the dark suite and letting the door close behind her.

When she heard it click, she let out the breath she'd been holding, dropped the flashlight into her pocket and began to casually stroll to the end of the hall.

Brody was at his post. "I don't even wanna know."

"You're right. You don't." Millie squeezed Brody's arm. "We should have lunch sometime soon so we can catch up. You can tell me how your new job is working out and if you've found a girlfriend yet."

"Now you sound like my sister, always trying to find me a girlfriend."

"There's nothing wrong with that." She slipped past Brody. "Thanks for the cover. We're just about even now."

Brody snorted. "Fat chance. I'm sure you'll think of something else."

Millie winked and turned to go.

"I hope you found whatever you were looking for."

"I didn't, but maybe that's a good thing." Millie thanked Brody again and then wandered down the steps.

During her rounds, Millie mulled over Brigitte Perez Bealitz. Perhaps Millie was overthinking the whole thing. She didn't have a shred of evidence Brigitte was involved in the art theft. Although she had a rap sheet, petty theft was a completely different ballgame than someone who heisted expensive artwork.

According to Josh, Teddy was feeling better. There was always the possibility he had feigned an illness in an attempt to gain his father's attention.

Looming large in Millie's mind was how to approach Danvers about marrying Nic. She could just sit back and let Captain Armati take the lead. The captain of the ship had more pull than she did.

Millie ended her rounds by checking with the excursion desk to make sure all booked excursions were wrapping up since it was getting late and began to make her way to the buffet area.

"Millie, are you there?" It was Sharky.

Millie plucked her radio from her belt and pressed the side button. "Go ahead Sharky."

"I got a hot one. You gotta get down here."

"I'm on my way." Millie darted to the lower deck and Sharky's office. She tapped on the door and then opened it.

Sharky was standing in front of his desk, his hand on top of a brown shipping box. "Is this what you're lookin' for?"

"Maybe." Millie hurried to his side and peered over his shoulder as she inspected the box marked "Fragile." "Where did you get this?"

"Kimel Pang brought it down here a little while ago. Hand delivered by the head of housekeeping. Must be pretty important." Sharky pointed to a garment bag draped over his office chair. "It fell out of the bottom of this garment bag."

"Can we open and re-seal it?" Millie asked.

"Are you kiddin'?" Sharky gasped. "We might as well throw ourselves overboard." He made a slicing motion across his neck. "Pang told me this bag belongs to the boss's girlfriend and to handle it with kid gloves. Besides, I'm waiting on Patterson. He's on his way."

Patterson arrived moments later. He didn't say a word but instead, walked over to the box and studied the front. "Where did you get this?"

"Kimel Pang, the head of housekeeping." Sharky went on to explain that Kimel arrived with a garment bag and a large suitcase, that the CEO of the company asked to have the items stored in the luggage area, explaining he planned to pick them up when he exited the ship Saturday morning. "He made a point of telling me the garment bag and suitcase belonged to the head honcho, Daniels, or something."

"Danvers," Patterson corrected. He pointed to the garment bag. "You say the box fell from the bottom of this bag?"

"Yep." Sharky nodded. "Kimel handed it to me and since he made such a big deal of who it belonged to, I wanted to double check everything. That's when the box fell out. The bottom of the bag was unzipped." He tapped the top of the box. "It looked kinda suspicious so I called you."

Patterson inspected the tag on the garment bag. "And Millie?"

"I called her too," Sharky said. "We have a deal."

The office door flew open and Kimel Pang ran into the room. "I need the garment bag back."

"It's over there." Sharky pointed to the garment bag still draped over the chair.

Kimel sprinted around the desk, unzipped the bag and began digging around inside. "There's a box." He turned to Sharky. "Remember the box that fell out of the bag?"

"This box?" Patterson pointed at the box on the desk.

"Yes." Kimel stepped over to the desk. "Mr. Danvers, he put the box inside the garment bag before I bring it down here but the missus, she mad because he not supposed to put it in bag. It belong to her."

"I see." Patterson picked up the box. "Kimel, you carry the garment bag and the two of us will head upstairs to return the box and the bag to the Mr. Danvers' suite."

"You're just going to leave us hanging?" Millie gasped.

"I'm sure you'll find out soon enough," Patterson said.

After Patterson and Kimel left, Sharky turned to Millie. "What's so all-fired important inside that small box that has all of you going berserk?"

"Art."

"Art?" Sharky asked incredulously. "The way everyone is acting, I thought it was the crown jewels."

"Close. Thanks for the heads up Sharky."

Millie headed to the lido deck. Her stomach began to grumble and she realized the only thing she'd eaten since early morning was the breakfast sandwich and she was starving.

She grabbed two slices of pepperoni pizza and zigzagged to the other side of the dining room where she found an empty table in the corner.

Millie bowed her head and prayed over her food, adding a special prayer that the mystery of the missing artwork was finally solved. She picked up a slice of pizza and nibbled the end, wondering how Danielle's date was going. She also wondered how Teddy and Josh were doing. Last, but not least, she wished she knew if Patterson, along with Danvers and Brigitte, had opened the box.

With Danielle off for the day, Millie was short-staffed so she hosted a round of trivia and finished up just in time to run to the theater for a few bingo sessions. After bingo, she headed to the gangway to greet the passengers who began making their way back on board the ship.

Danielle and Stephen Chow were among the first to return to the ship. Millie smiled as she caught a glimpse of Danielle's flushed cheeks. "I'll be right back," the young woman promised breathlessly.

"I'll be here."

Danielle returned a short time later, dressed in uniform and just in time for a long line of passengers to begin boarding. Thankfully, embarkation went off without a hitch and the ship set sail right on schedule.

The rest of the day flew by and Millie went to bed that night wondering what had happened with the box and anxious to start her last full day with Danvers on board.

Unlike the previous morning, Millie woke early and bounded out of bed. It was the last full day of the cruise and the captain's dinner was that evening. Captain Armati, along with Millie, Donovan Sweeney, Staff Captain Antonio Vitale and the Danvers' party would be dining together that evening.

Millie vowed that nothing was going to get her down. Her first priority of the day was to chat with Josh, and they met in front of the employee lounge. "How is Teddy?"

"He's back to 100% with no complaints of feeling ill. There's something else." Josh waited for several crewmembers to pass by. "I'm heading up there shortly. Did you hear?"

Millie leaned closer. "Hear what?"

"Teddy told me Danvers kicked Brigitte out of their suite. She's staying in an inside cabin on deck three. When I took him back to the suite last night, Brigitte was gone and when I asked, Teddy told me his father ended their relationship."

Millie's eyes widened. "Wow."

"He's not sure what happened, but Brigitte is gone and Teddy is, of course, thrilled."

Millie thanked Josh for the information and they parted ways on deck nine where Josh and Teddy planned to meet in the arcade.

"I can't stand it any longer," Millie muttered under her breath.

When she reached Patterson's office, she could see the lights were on so she tapped lightly on the door and then barged into the room. "What happened?"

"It's nice to see you, too, Millie." Patterson looked up from his computer.

"Well?"

"Well what?" Patterson asked.

"The box. What happened with the box?"

"Oh. That."

"Stop messing with me." Millie flopped down in an empty chair.

"Kimel and I took the garment bag and the box to the Danvers' suite where a panicked Brigitte answered the door. When she saw the box, she tried to take it from me. I asked her to open it and she started screaming that if I didn't give it to her, she was going to have me fired."

"Did you give it back to her?"

"Danvers was there. He overheard our conversation and told me to open it."

Millie sucked in a breath. "The painting was in there."

"Yes," Patterson nodded. "One of the missing pieces of art was inside."

"I knew it." Millie slammed an open palm on Patterson's desk.

"I've already spoken with Stanley Zelchon and he's going to meet with his boss to decide whether or not they are going to press charges against Ms. Perez Bealitz."

"Stanley Zelchon? I would think Brenda Parcore would be in charge of that," Millie said.

"Zelchon is a close friend of the owner of High Seas Gallery. The owner suspected Brenda Parcore was selling the auctioned art under market value so, as a personal favor, Zelchon offered to come on board to try to figure out what was going on. When the artwork went missing, Brenda was officially under internal investigation."

"Ah." Millie lifted a brow. "I always thought it was suspicious that Zelchon would leave a prestigious job to come work on our cruise ship."

Patterson shifted in his chair. "So now you've got another notch in your sleuthing belt," he teased. "Although High Seas couldn't have pinned the thefts on you or Andy. They had no proof."

"True, but who needs a lingering question mark hanging over their head?"

Millie scooched out of the chair and slowly stood. "Now I've only got one more teensy problem to resolve."

"Let me guess. It's Captain Armati's plan to present the crew and staff's petition to Mr. Danvers this evening at dinner."

"What do you think will happen?"

Patterson shrugged. "Danvers is hard to read. I have no idea."

She thought of Teddy's unexplained illnesses. "I do have one more thing to throw out there but it's just a suspicion."

"I can't wait to hear it."

Millie shared with Patterson her suspicions that someone...Brigitte, may have poisoned Teddy in an attempt to get rid of him. "Or perhaps she needed someone to guard the suite and Teddy was an easy target."

Patterson lifted a brow. "That's a stretch, Millie."

"True. The fact Brigitte insisted Kimel, the head of housekeeping, clean their suite and that she be present whenever he was in the suite is suspect. Plus, who places security guards at the end of the hall?"

"The CEO of the cruise line." Patterson shook his head. "It's all speculation, Millie. It appears Brigitte is out of the picture regardless so Teddy is safe."

Millie thanked Patterson for the update and walked to the door.

"Don't you want to know *how* Brigitte heisted the artwork?" Patterson asked.

"Of course. I guess I'm losing my touch. How did she get her hands on the artwork?"

"Finally, I have one on you." Patterson tapped the side of his forehead. "Even after we opened the box Brigitte refused to confess, so Oscar and I took another look inside the gallery. The first clue was that all of the paintings had been stolen from the display cases inside the gallery."

"Out of sight," Millie quipped.

"Yes, out of sight but still accessible. After examining the special cases, we discovered we could easily open the cases using this." Patterson reached inside his front pocket, pulled out a multi tool pocketknife and flipped it open. "See this?"

"Yeah." Millie nodded.

"Oscar and I were able to open the display cases with these spring action needle nose pliers." Patterson closed the knife and shoved it back inside his pocket. "You can imagine the look on Parcore and Zelchon's faces when I showed them how easy their state-of-the-art, impenetrable display cases were to open."

"I'll bet." Millie shook her head. "I'm sure they'll be changing those out faster than you can say high seas heist."

"And locking the gallery doors when it's not open," Patterson said. "After interviewing Danvers, we pieced together the events. Brigitte excused herself after the tour Friday night and we believe that's when she made her way into the gallery, opened the cases and slipped the artwork into her oversized tote bag."

"Ah." Millie lifted a brow. "She walked right off the cruise ship with them in her bag. When Danvers, Teddy and she boarded Saturday morning for the weeklong cruise, the temptation was too much so she stole another piece."

"The fact that Kimel Pang was the only one allowed inside the suite and under Brigitte's direct supervision leads me to believe she hid the last piece of stolen art in the suite. Brigitte was at the spa when Kimel showed up to take the large suitcase full of clothes and one of the garment bags to the below deck storage area."

Patterson went on to tell Millie that the box was sitting next to the garment bag and Danvers placed it inside the bag. "He was in a hurry, shoved it inside the garment bag and didn't notice it wasn't zipped all the way shut."

Patterson continued. "After Kimel handed off the two pieces of luggage to Sharky, he returned to the Danvers' suite. Brigitte was in an uproar, screaming at both Danvers and Kimel that she never told them to take the box and insisting Kimel track it down."

"So I only solved half the crime," Millie teased. "I better step up my game or I'll be out of my moonlighting job."

Patterson rolled his eyes. "I can only dream of the day when you don't stick your nose in every single one of my investigations."

Chapter 22

"The outfit looks fine," Danielle said.

Millie shifted to the right, smoothed the front of her skirt and eyed herself critically in the mirror. "Are you sure? I can change back into the periwinkle maxi dress. It matches my eyes."

"You look fabulous." Danielle placed her hand on Millie's back and propelled her toward the cabin door. "If you don't hustle, you're gonna be late."

Millie reached for her lanyard and slipped it into her front pocket. "Wish me luck."

"You don't need luck. I'm sure you'll charm the pants off Danvers."

"He can keep his pants on. All he needs to do is give Nic and me his blessing."

"You know what I mean." Danielle opened up the door and shooed Millie into the hall before closing the door behind her.

Millie glanced at the door, sucked in a deep breath and hurried down the hall, all the while praying that somehow, some way Danvers would agree to let the captain and her marry and stay on board the Siren of the Seas together.

She was the last to arrive at the captain's table and the only woman. The men, including Teddy, stood until Captain Armati pulled out Millie's chair and she was seated. "You look ravishing," he whispered under his breath.

"T-thank you," Millie stuttered. It was going to be a very long evening.

Thankfully, the men kept the conversation going, which was all one-sided and focused on Danvers and the cruise ship industry. He made several suggestions and some of them were sound advice.

Millie began to relax until dessert and coffee arrived. She glanced worriedly at Captain Armati and he tried to give her a reassuring smile, but she could see he was anxious, as well. Their future hinged on Danvers' decision.

Millie's armpits grew damp and she nervously sipped her coffee. She took one bite of the cherry cheesecake before pushing it aside.

After the wait staff removed the dessert dishes, their waiter offered each of them hard candies from a dish. Millie slipped one of the mints in her mouth, hoping it would settle her churning stomach.

Teddy passed on the candies but his father took two, unwrapped them and popped both of them in his mouth.

Captain Armati gave Millie a quick glance, cleared his throat and stood. "Mr. Danvers, we have truly enjoyed having you on board Siren of the Seas this week." He reached inside his jacket and pulled out a stack of stapled sheets of paper...the petition.

"As you may remember, and I mentioned in an email some time ago, I proposed to Ms. Sanders.

We plan to marry soon and would like to stay on board Siren of the Seas as husband and wife."

Danvers started to speak, but Captain Armati pressed on. "The staff and crew on board the ship have signed a petition in support of this request."

"I don't..." Danvers shifted in his seat and sucked in a breath. His eyes began to bulge and he clutched his throat as he looked around the table frantically.

Millie realized with horror that the hard candy had somehow lodged in his throat. Danvers was choking!

She sprang from her chair and raced to the other side of the table. By then, Danvers was on his feet so she slipped behind him and wrapped her arms around his waist. Millie made a fist with one hand, placing the thumb side of her fist against his stomach.

She grasped her fist with the other hand and, with as much force as she could muster, thrust upward.

The first time she pressed into his abdomen, nothing happened.

Panic started to set in. Millie took a quick breath and using every ounce of her strength, tried the Heimlich maneuver again.

The candy flew out of Danvers' mouth, bounced across the table and rolled onto the floor.

Danvers bent forward, gasping for air.

Teddy jumped out of his chair. "Dad, are you okay?"

Danvers nodded, rubbing his throat with one hand and patting his son's shoulder with the other. "Yes son. I'm okay." He swiped at his watery eyes and turned to Millie. "You've got some muscle on you, Millie. Thank you."

"Y-you're welcome. I'm sorry if I hurt you."

The waiter rushed to bring a glass of water and the surrounding tables began to applaud Millie's valiant lifesaving effort. She smiled faintly before resuming her place at the table.

Danvers cleared his throat. "Now where were we? Oh, the wedding. You know the company policy and if you two wed, policy states you're not allowed to remain on the same ship." His voice trailed off as he gazed at the somber faces around the table.

"Dad," Teddy said. "Millie saved your life."

Danvers slowly nodded. His eyes met Millie's eyes. "However, policies can change, depending on circumstances." He paused. "I'll have to present the request to the board of directors for final approval...but I think I can get it pushed through."

Millie let out the breath she'd been holding and clutched her chest as tears filled her eyes.

Captain Armati shoved his chair back and sprang to his feet. He pulled his bride-to-be out of her chair and into his arms. "I guess there's no escaping me now."

The last thing Millie heard before Nic bent down to kiss her was the thundering roar of applause.

The end.

If you enjoyed reading "High Seas Heist," please take a moment to leave a review. It would be greatly appreciated! Thank you!

The Series Continues...Book 11 in the "Cruise Ship Cozy Mysteries" Series Coming Soon!

List of Hope Callaghan Books
(Read FREE In Kindle Unlimited)

Made in Savannah Cozy Mystery Series

Key to Savannah: Book 1
Road to Savannah: Book 2
Justice in Savannah: Book 3
Swag in Savannah: Book 4
Trouble in Savannah: Book 5
Missing in Savannah: Book 6 (New Release)
Book 7: Coming Soon!

Garden Girls Cozy Mystery Series

Who Murdered Mr. Malone? Book 1
Grandkids Gone Wild: Book 2
Smoky Mountain Mystery: Book 3
Death by Dumplings: Book 4
Eye Spy: Book 5
Magnolia Mansion Mysteries: Book 6
Missing Milt: Book 7
Bully in the 'Burbs: Book 8
Fall Girl: Book 9
Home for the Holidays: Book 10
Sun, Sand, and Suspects: Book 11
Look Into My Ice: Book 12
Forget Me Knot: Book 13
Nightmare in Nantucket: Book 14
Greed with Envy: Book 15

Dying for Dollars: Book 16
Book 17: Coming Soon!
Garden Girls Box Set I – (Books 1-3)
Garden Girls Box Set II – (Books 4-6)

Cruise Ship Cozy Mystery Series

Starboard Secrets: Book 1
Portside Peril: Book 2
Lethal Lobster: Book 3
Deadly Deception: Book 4
Vanishing Vacationers: Book 5
Cruise Control: Book 6
Killer Karaoke: Book 7
Suite Revenge: Book 8
Cruisin' for a Bruisin': Book 9
High Seas Heist: Book 10 (New Release!)
Book 11: Coming Soon!
Cruise Ship Cozy Mysteries Box Set I (Books 1-3)
Cruise Ship Cozy Mysteries Box Set II (Books 4-6)

Sweet Southern Sleuths Cozy Mysteries
Short Stories Series

Teepees and Trailer Parks: Book 1
Bag of Bones: Book 2
Southern Stalker: Book 3
Two Settle the Score: Book 4
Killer Road Trip: Book 5
Pups in Peril: Book 6

Dying To Get Married-In: Book 7
Deadly Drive-In: Book 8
Secrets of a Stranger: Book 9
Library Lockdown: Book 10
Vandals & Vigilantes: Book 11
Fatal Frolic: Book 12
Sweet Southern Sleuths Box Set I: (Books 1-4)
Sweet Southern Sleuths Box Set: II: (Books 5-8)
Sweet Southern Sleuths Box Set III: (Books 9-12)
Sweet Southern Sleuths 12 Book Box Set (Entire Series)

Samantha Rite Deception Mystery Series

Waves of Deception: Book 1
Winds of Deception: Book 2
Tides of Deception: Book 3
Samantha Rite Series Box Set – (Books 1-3-The Complete Series)

Get Free Books and More!

Sign up for my Free Cozy Mystery Newsletter to get free and discounted ebooks, giveaways & soon-to-be-released books!

hopecallaghan.com/newsletter

Meet the Author

Hope Callaghan is an author who loves to write Christian books, especially Christian Mystery and Cozy Mystery books. She has written more than 50 mystery books (and counting) in five series.

In March 2017, Hope won a Mom's Choice Award for her book, "Key to Savannah," Book 1 in the Made in Savannah Cozy Mystery Series.

Born and raised in a small town in West Michigan, she now lives in Florida with her husband.

She is the proud mother of one daughter and a stepdaughter and stepson. When she's not doing the thing she loves best - writing books - she enjoys cooking, traveling and reading books.

Hope loves to connect with her readers! Connect with her today!

Visit **hopecallaghan.com** for special offers, free books, and soon-to-be-released books!

Email: hope@hopecallaghan.com

**Facebook:
https://www.facebook.com/hopecallaghan author/**

Wet Burrito Recipe

Ingredients:
1 lb. ground beef (can substitute ground chicken or turkey)
½ cup chopped yellow onion
1 tsp. cumin
½ tsp. salt
½ tsp. pepper
1 – 4.5 oz. can diced green chile peppers
1 – 16 oz. can refried beans
1 – 10 oz. can rotel
1 – 10 oz. can enchilada sauce
4 – 8 inch flour tortillas
2 cups shredded lettuce
1 cup chopped tomatoes
2 cups shredded Mexican cheese
½ cup chopped green onion

Directions:
-Cook ground meat over medium high heat until browned. Add onion. Cook and stir until the onion is translucent. Drain grease, if necessary.
-Season with cumin, salt and pepper. Stir thoroughly.
-Stir in green chile and refried beans until blended. Remove from heat.
-In a small saucepan, combine rotel and enchilada sauce. Heat thoroughly.
-Place a warm tortilla on plate. Spoon ¼ of the

meat mixture along center of tortilla.

-Top with lettuce and tomato.

-Roll tortilla.

-Spoon a generous amount of sauce over top of rolled burrito.

-Sprinkle cheese and scallion over top of sauce.

-Heat in microwave for 30 seconds, or until cheese melts.

-Repeat steps for other three tortillas.

Sharky's Atomic Salsa Recipe

NOTE. The original recipe called for ghost peppers. Ghost peppers can be lethal so I substituted the ghost pepper with jalapeno.

Ingredients:
1 jalapeno, diced
4 chopped/drained tomatoes
1 bunch green onions, chopped
1 small can black olives, chopped
1 small can green chiles, chopped
1 clove garlic, minced
1 tbsp olive oil
1 tsp. white vinegar
¼ cup water
Salt and pepper to taste

Directions:
-Mix ingredients.
-Refrigerate one hour or for best flavor, overnight.
-Serve with chips

Made in the USA
Columbia, SC
05 June 2024